Never Been Born

KIMBERLY HAMMER

Dedication

For Ryan, who blessed many with his infectious smile
and outpouring of love. Your memory lives on.

Special thanks and appreciation go to
Ramy Vance for his writing guidance and to
Shavonne Clarke for her editing expertise.

Introduction

each life is a story waiting to unfold. Let the Lord write
the chapters of your life and the ending will be divine.
Think of the special people in your life—you know, the
ones who hold you close when you're at your lowest point and
the ones who celebrate life's successes with you. Now imagine
what your life would have been like if they had never been born.

> "For you created my inmost being; you knit me together
> in my mother's womb." Psalm 139:13

Chapter 1

*G*ina Martin should have been the one lying in Larson's Funeral Home. Words could not describe the utter grief that consumed her. She had heard of others losing a child, but it happened to *others,* not to herself. Everyone knows that children aren't supposed to die before their parents. Why hadn't it been her instead of her only son?

Being a teacher, June days were ones Gina daydreamed about months in advance. However, this would be a June like no other, and one that would forever change the course of Gina's life.

On that day, school had just let out for summer. The days ahead beckoned to Gina with their endless possibilities. She thought of the garden she had all but ignored with the busyness of May. How Gina longed to have cosmos, pansies and snapdragons brandishing their colors once again. Her garden brought joy and serenity to her busy life. Hiking the various trails of Mt. Tamalpais would enable her to decompress after the stress of this past school year. Teaching second graders, while rewarding, brought many challenges. Or, she could finally finish the oil painting that languished on its easel in her back bedroom. So many choices, but grading papers was one choice she did not have to consider.

Gina continued to sip her coffee while contemplating how to spend the day before her. Her thoughts wandered to Abby, her best friend. Gina really should call her. They had chatted about spending a few days near Big Sur. Their lives always seemed to be in a constant whirl of activity, and little time remained to just enjoy each other's friendship. A chance to get away would be heavenly. They could wander around the small town of Cambria, visit a few art galleries, and have some scrumptious dinners. Gina's mouth started watering at the thought of the crab cakes she had enjoyed on her last visit to Cambria.

Life wasn't always like this. Gina remembered many summers when Abby and her son, Peter, would join Gina and her son, Mattie, on weeklong camping trips in northern California. They hiked, swam, and enjoyed leisurely campfires into the wee hours of the night. Oh, the burnt fingers and scorched marshmallows that accompanied those campfires always brought a laugh or two. How Gina missed those days. Both boys were long grown and living their own lives. Isn't that the way it's supposed to be?

The ringing of Gina's cell phone interrupted her musings. Picking it up, she hoped it wasn't another telemarketer; their constant harassment wearied her. "Hello."

"Gina, it's Emma," came a strained voice. "Hi, Emma! How are things going?"

"Gina, it's about Mattie … I have something to tell you. He … There was a car accident … Mattie's gone. I'm so sorry."

"Emma, what are you talking about?" Gina's voice seemed to rise in volume.

"Mattie had an early morning meeting in Sacramento. He was driving on Highway 70 when a drunk driver hit him head on. The CHP said Mattie probably died on impact. Mattie's gone!" Emma sobbed into the phone.

"No! It can't be! Not Mattie!" Gina screamed. "Emma, you must be mistaken. I just spoke with him yesterday!"

"Gina, I wish it wasn't true," Emma sobbed. "He meant everything to me. We were just beginning to plan our future together—Mattie, Travis, and me."

The cell phone clattered to the floor, and Gina crumpled into a heap beside it. Her cries sounded something like those of a wounded animal. She clasped her arms around herself and wailed until it seemed like there were neither breath nor tears left in her body. How long she remained like that, Gina didn't know.

Why had her son been snatched away from her at such a young age? His life was just beginning. She had experienced so much in her fifty years and would gladly trade places with him. It should have been her in that car, not him. How senseless life often seemed to be, and to think it was a drunk driver who took Mattie's life. Gina would ensure that this drunk would never have the opportunity to take another life.

Pulling herself off the floor, Gina moved with numbness to the bathroom. She dabbed her red, swollen eyes with a tissue, trying to erase the mascara stain that streamed down her face.

Blowing her dripping nose, Gina noted that it seemed twice its usual size. After splashing cold water on her face, she retreated to the couch to begin a reverie of sorts. Her thoughts transported her back to twenty-five years earlier, seemingly a lifetime ago. Back then, she'd been terrified of one one thing: becoming pregnant.

Chapter 2

*G*ina sat looking at the results of the pregnancy kit. How could they be positive? How had this happened? A knot formed within her stomach, and panic was beginning to well up inside her. There is no way she wanted another obstacle to overcome in what was already a complicated relationship. She would tell Bryan; he deserved to know, being the father of this child. Somehow she sensed that he would insist upon her terminating the pregnancy. Sighing, Gina realized that she didn't have much choice in what needed to be done. Nevertheless, Gina felt a twinge of regret for all the possibilities that little life represented. She twisted her auburn ponytail between her fingers as the panic within her continued to mount.

Gina had met Bryan through a mutual friend. He seemed to possess the qualities that she lacked. Being naturally outgoing, people were drawn to him by his wit and charm. She, too, found those qualities about him irresistible. While Gina was more of an introvert, somehow they had connected. Before long, Bryan suggested they move in together. They found a small, yet still expensive apartment near where they both worked. What fun they had furnishing it, though Bryan insisted on keeping things simple; he didn't want any feminine touches which might suggest a real home. Gina didn't truly care. It was Bryan her heart longed for.

They had been living together for just a few months. Bryan made it clear on several occasions that this arrangement was nothing permanent; rather, let's "wait and see where this relationship goes." Bryan's career as a sales manager was beginning to show promise, and Gina had recently landed a job teaching second grade. Their lives and relationship were unsettled at best. How could this inconvenience have happened?

When Gina did tell Bryan about her pregnancy, he came unglued, and his eyes flashed in anger. "What the hell are you talking about—you're pregnant? I thought you were on the pill? You will take care of this."

"Bryan, I'm sorry. It was an accident. I'm not sure how it happened." Gina felt like she had to defend herself against his accusations.

"An accident, really?" he questioned, glaring at her.

Gina sat shell-shocked at his tirade. She didn't plan on having a baby, but Bryan's anger and vehemence unsettled her. Couldn't he see how torn she felt?

Gina called her lifelong friend, Abby. Gina cried into the phone, pouring out the situation to her. "Abby, he wouldn't even listen! He's convinced that I deliberately became pregnant to trap him into a permanent relationship. I'm so angry, but I'm also hurt," Gina sobbed.

After listening for some time, Abby interrupted Gina by asking, "What do you want?"

A long silence ensued. Gina replied, "I don't know. I had never even thought about something like this happening. I'm devastated by Bryan's response. He looks at me with such anger and suspicion. I don't know if our relationship can be salvaged, even if I go ahead with the abortion like he insists."

"Gina, you know that I love you. Don't make a decision just now. Give yourself a little time to mull things over, but most of all, follow your heart. I will support whatever you decide to do."

"I suppose you're right." As Gina hung up the phone, she felt like at least one person believed her.

❯❯❯❯❯ ❮❮❮❮❮

Gina thought back to that moment twenty-five years ago and the decision she had to make. It wasn't easy. How she wanted a life together with Bryan, yet something inside her cried out for that tiny being as well. Would things have turned out differently with Bryan had she made another choice? *I suppose I'll never know. Does it matter now? I've lost everything that gave my life meaning.* Tears streamed down her face once more.

❯❯❯❯❯ ❮❮❮❮❮

Nine months after discovering she was pregnant, Gina gazed at the small bundle cradled in her arms. The blue eyes were closed in absolute peace while the tiny fingers grasped each other. She had never seen a more perfect baby. While her pregnancy had not been an easy one, the pain quickly faded from memory upon meeting her wee son. "You are such a beautiful boy, my little Mattie."

Mattie brought her so much joy with his gurgles and coos. How could she ever have considered him not being a part of her life? Gina held him close, listening to the soft sounds he made. Things almost turned out differently as she thought back to that fateful decision. "You are my sweet boy, aren't you?" she murmured as she stroked his fair hair. While Gina had never pictured herself as a mother, things changed once that little one entered her life.

⟫⟫⟩ ⟨⟪⟪

Children are not supposed to die before their parents. That was a given. Rising from the couch where Gina had spent the past two hours grieving, she shook her fists and raged against an unseen person. "God, why him? His life was just beginning. He had found the love of his life. He was good and kind. Lord, why? Explain it to me, because I don't understand!" She broke into sobs once more. "Why give him to me so long ago only to yank him away now?"

Gina picked up a nearby photo of baby Mattie. Her thoughts traveled back to those early days. She had just started her teaching career. Being pregnant and single was frowned upon; nevertheless, the school where Gina taught allowed her to take three months off for maternity leave. How she would manage finances with the added expense of daycare, Gina didn't know. Bryan would be of no help. He had never inquired as to how she was doing throughout her pregnancy. Somehow *she* would make it work.

Once Mattie arrived, Gina wanted nothing more than to enjoy her little one and being a mom. Her own mother and friends helped out by watching him, preparing meals, and giving her a break whenever they could. It wasn't easy being a single mom or returning to work with a baby, but each day brought new experiences as Mattie grew and changed.

Chapter 3

*G*ina retrieved her cell phone from the kitchen floor. Glancing at the time, she realized that a mere three hours had passed since Emma's phone call. Gina needed to share her heartache with the one person who would also feel her loss; she pressed Abby's number. When her friend answered, Gina cried in to the phone, "Abby, he's gone! Mattie's gone!"

"Gina, what are you talking about?"

Gina related the earlier phone call from Emma with the details of the accident.

"Gina, you understand that you need to go up to Chico right away.

You will have to begin making arrangements for Mattie. You can't expect Emma to handle that."

Between sobs, Gina said, "I can't. That will make things so... so final! I can't accept that he's gone, that he's not coming back."

"Honey, I understand. I'll go with you. How about tomorrow? I'll talk to my boss and arrange to take a few days off. We will take care of this together."

"You're probably right."

"Gina, I love you. I'm here for you. You know that."

"I know. Thank you."

❯❯❯❯❯ ❮❮❮❮❮

Gina thought about how quickly that time had passed with her little one. Others had warned her that would happen once she became a mom, but Gina never fully understood it until later in life. How she adored him. Becoming a mother gave her a capacity to love another in a way she had never thought possible.

Before she knew it, Mattie was crawling, then toddling around. Where had these past few months gone? Each evening they had their special routine before Gina laid him down for bed. After dinner and a bath, she hoisted Mattie up on her knees as he flew through the air.

"He flies through the air with the greatest of ease, it's Matthew P. Hensley on the flying trapeze," Gina sang out. Mattie let out squeals of laughter along with "more!"

The ride was followed by a story that Gina usually had to read at least two times. Of course Mattie was always in the story in some form, whether he was the little boy, a farmer, or a truck named Mattie.

Finally, there was rocking and lots of hugs and kisses before he was laid down for the night. He was her sweet boy. While the days seemed endless with teaching and caring for Mattie, Gina realized that this was indeed the best time of her life.

❖❖❖❖ ❖❖❖❖

"Life isn't supposed to be like this," Gina reasoned, climbing into bed that night. "There is an order to the universe, or at least there's supposed to be; one where parents grow *old* while children merely become older." Sleep was hard to come by with such sorrow weighing on her heart.

Gina found herself enveloped by a mist. She could barely distinguish the outlines of trees, tall grass, and a path leading into a forest. Through the gloom, she glimpsed Mattie walking toward the woodland. She called out to him, but her words seemed to be lost in the heavy air surrounding her. Gina willed her body to move, to try to reach him, yet she couldn't. Mattie turned to look at her before he dissolved into the mist.

Awakening with her heart pounding within her chest and her breath coming in short gasps, Gina peered around the room anxiously. She spied moonlight filtering in through the sheer window coverings and nothing more. Her body relaxed a bit until she remembered Mattie. He had been there. She had tried to reach him, to call out to him before he disappeared. It was a dream, but then again, it wasn't. He had vanished before she could tell him goodbye.

Turning over in bed, Gina pondered the futility of life as tears once more slid down her face. It seemed that just when you figured things out, life threw you a curveball. All the years she spent raising Mattie by herself and never marrying. She often wondered whether she had succeeded in laying the foundation her son would need as an adult. Had it all been for naught?

Bryan came to mind. *I'll have to let him know about Mattie's passing regardless of my own feelings,* Gina thought. Bryan had never been much of a father to Mattie. The time he spent with Mattie was hit or miss. Bryan would arrange to see Mattie on a particular day; it might be months before he would call again. There was no consistency, and eventually Mattie realized that Bryan's relationship with him was more that of a friend than a father.

Gina learned that Bryan had eventually married. No mention was ever made of children, so she suspected that he remained childless. Bryan's affairs were of little interest to her, so she paid scant attention to any comments about him that might come her way.

⋙ ⋘

Gina woke the following morning, her mind a bit fuzzy. Heaviness weighed on her heart; then she remembered the source of that weight—Mattie, her son, was gone. Gina knew that Abby would be arriving soon for them to make their trek to Chico. Gina wanted to remain hidden under the covers. The thought of trying to get out of bed and face the day was almost too much to bear. Gina willed herself to get up, shower, and dress. It took all the strength she could muster to perform those tasks. Numbly she threw a few items in an overnight bag, not thinking or caring about what she was packing.

Abby arrived at 9:00 that morning; after loading her car, they set off on the four-hour drive from the Bay Area to Chico. Mattie had fallen in love with the community years ago while attending college. He continued to live there, and Gina knew that Chico had become home to him. His friends were more family than merely friends.

"Abby, I'm so grateful that you're here with me. I couldn't do this without you."

"Gina, you know that Mattie was like a son to me. All the time we spent together with the kids—Boy Scouts, trips to the beach, the mountains. I wouldn't have it any other way."

Gina dabbed at her eyes as the tears began to flow once more. "It's okay, honey. You're allowed to cry. Let it all out."

"I miss him so much! We spoke Sunday night on the phone, and he had such exuberance in his voice."

"Hey, Mom, it's Mattie," he'd said that Sunday. "I want to share some great news with you. Emma and I are taking Travis up to Lake Tahoe in two weeks. While there, I plan to propose to Emma."

"Mattie, that's wonderful! I'm beyond excited for you and Emma!"

"So am I. Emma is an amazing woman, and Travis is a pretty cool five-year-old."

"Oh honey, I can hardly wait to have him for a grandson!'

Mattie laughed. "Well, you're going to have to wait a few months."

"Can't I begin practicing now?"

"Of course."

"Give Emma my love. I'm so thrilled for both of you!"

"Will do." And the conversation ended.

Gina turned to Abby in the car. "Their future was just beginning. Why? Why do these things happen? Explain it me!" demanded Gina as tears flowed down her cheeks.

"Gina, I don't have the answer for that. None of us understands it. Hold onto your memories of him and the love in your heart. That's all I can say." Abby reached over and grabbed Gina's hand. "It's okay to let it out. Scream, shake your fists at Heaven; do whatever you need to if it helps."

"I may do that. Hope you brought ear plugs along." That brought a smile to both of their faces.

"Have you spoken with Bryan about Mattie?"

Gina let out an audible breath.. "I called him earlier this morning at work. He's usually at his desk by 8:00. I figured by calling him there I could keep the conversation brief. It worked."

"How did he take the news?" Abby asked.

"He didn't say much; he was kind of quiet. He said to let him know the day and location of anything we planned for Mattie, and he would be there."

"Wow—when was the last time you spoke with him?"

Gina sighed, "The last time I saw or spoke with him was atMattie's graduation in Chico three years ago. He came by himself. His wife didn't join him."

"Gina, I'm sorry that you have to deal with him on top of everything else. It doesn't seem fair."

"Mattie did care about Bryan, even though Bryan wasn't consistently in Mattie's life. I vacillated between being grateful for that as well as feeling angry. Bryan seemed so engrossed in his own affairs I felt that any influence he would exert on Mattie would be less than positive, yet I knew that Mattie longed to know his dad and have a relationship with him."

Abby nodded her head knowingly. "You know full well all I went through with my divorce from Michael. It's never easy dealing with an ex-spouse. You have the parenting decisions, trying to arrange a holiday schedule, not to mention the visitation issues. At least you were spared from that."

Chapter 4

mma greeted Gina and Abby at the door of her early 1920s style home. While Gina had met Emma previously, she felt an immediate camaraderie over their shared loss. Gina noticed that Emma's grief was as deep as her own by her red swollen eyes and disheveled appearance. The two women embraced. "Come on in," Emma gestured.

"This is my best friend, Abby," Gina said, pointing to Abby.

"I'm so sorry for your loss. Mattie was like a son to me. Words are inadequate at a time like this," Abby said, hugging Emma.

Gina glanced around the small but cozy living room. Cars and trucks of all sizes were piled in a large basket in one corner. In another corner, an unfinished Lego creation sat on a pint-sized table with an assortment of books and smaller toys nearby. Several pictures of Mattie, Emma, and Travis, Emma's young son, were arranged on the mantel. In one photo they appeared to be camping in the mountains, and in another they were attending an outdoor air show. Complete joy radiated from their faces.

Emma caught Gina gazing at the photo of the air show. "Mattie arranged that as a surprise for Travis's birthday. Travis talked about it for days! Did Mattie ever score points in Travis's opinion!" Emma wiped her eyes while looking away.

"It's clear that he loved you both very much."

"We felt the same way. Mattie changed our lives—both Travis's and mine. He gave us a fresh start, a new beginning."

"I'd like to hear about how you met."

"I'd be happy to tell you. Maybe later. We should probably head over to Larson's Funeral Home and go over some of the arrangements for Mattie. They do need your permission and signature for cremation."

At the word cremation, Gina was jerked back to reality.

Cremation. What an ugly word. It had such finality to it. The thought of her son as mere ashes was more than she could bear to think of.

"You probably want to see him one last time as well," Emma added.

"Emma, I don't. What lies in Larson's Funeral Home is not Mattie, but a shell. I want to remember him as the man he was—full of life, laughter, and love. Not something that has been cleaned up for family viewing. I thought about this on the drive up here. My last visit to Chico was magical. Mattie and I had a wonderful dinner at Tres Hombres and time together to discuss his plans for the future. I have never seen him so enthusiastic and passionate about the course he planned to follow. Part of that was due to you, I know." Emma nodded knowingly.

⋙ ⋘

Gina performed the tasks at Larson's Funeral Home in a perfunctory manner. Craig Larson, the funeral director, explained the paperwork that needed to be completed and filed with the state. He suggested other tasks Gina should handle as soon as possible such as canceling credit cards, insurance policies, and Mattie's driver license. Gina nearly had a panic attack as she thought of all she had to do. As Mattie had never married, it fell upon Gina to make the necessary decisions.

Internally, Gina screamed, *God, how can you allow this? Why? I don't understand. You are supposed to be a merciful God. Why didn't you show my son the same mercy that you've shown others?*

Craig Larson guided Gina through the rest of the process. Yes, Mattie would be cremated, then his ashes placed in an urn. Gina would hold a small ceremony the following week, which family and friends could attend. Abby and Emma promised to help with the latter.

Observing the drawn look on her friend's face, Abby urged, "Come on. You've had enough for one afternoon. Let's grab something to eat."

"That sounds good," agreed Emma. "Travis is with my mom, so I don't need to be home right away."

The trio headed to a small restaurant and settled in on the patio. Gina realized she hadn't eaten anything that day, and hunger pangs were gnawing at her. Glancing at the menu, she noted that the Asian chicken salad sounded good and decided upon it. The other women chose salads as well, the sweltering heat dampening their appetites.

"How about a glass of wine?" Abby asked, scanning the various selections.

"A great idea," agreed Gina. "I'm ready to drown my sorrows in a sea of forgetfulness."

Abby gave Gina a look suggesting, *don't even think about it.*

Sipping a glass of sangria, Emma said, "You asked me how Mattie and I met; well, this is the story of how he came into my life."

As they sat around the table sipping their wine, Emma explained that a mutual friend had introduced Mattie to Emma. They seemed to hit it off immediately. Emma had the same passion for life that he did. Her blue eyes sparkled as she talked, and her smile radiated a joy from deep within her. Mattie soon learned that Emma concealed much pain beneath that bright smile.

Emma married right out of high school to her sweetheart. At first, all had been well. But disillusionment soon set in. Emma's husband, Jake, had been very controlling. Emma had little time with friends or anyone outside Jake's sphere of influence. Even Emma's family soon became estranged.

Emma thought having a baby might help the marriage. Things improved, but not for long. Baby Travis was born four weeks early due to preeclampsia. Emma felt exhausted between the constant feedings and Travis's endless cries. Jake had little patience for the crying or the attention that Travis demanded. The bickering began once again, and Jake seemed to spend less time at home. While that might have appeared to be a blessing, he left Emma alone with the baby and without any transportation. Living in a remote area, Emma was isolated from others.

Once the days warmed a bit, Emma began taking Travis for long walks. One day that walk led into the small town of Pioneer. Emma pushed the stroller into the Easy Stop that was both a mini mart and gas station. She noticed a sign posted in the window: *Daycare Help Wanted.* That was something she could do while still caring for Travis. Emma walked inside the store.

"Hi. Can you tell me where I go to apply for the daycare job?"

The middle-aged man behind the counter peered at her and the baby in the stroller curiously. "Go down to Main Street. 211—it's the second building on the left-hand side of the street. Good luck to you," he said with a smile.

Emma continued down the road until she reached Main Street. Looking for 211, she spotted it, then pushed the stroller to a stop in front of the building. Removing Travis from the stroller, Emma carried him inside. She spied a woman in her forties sitting at a desk. The woman glanced up at Emma and Travis. "Can I help you?"

"Yes. I saw the ad about needing daycare help. I'd like to apply for the position."

The woman, Kris, asked Emma questions about her experience, availability, and Travis.

Emma desired the companionship of others, and she knew it would be healthy for Travis to be surrounded by children as well. After much discussion, Kris offered Emma the position to begin the following Monday. Emma thanked Kris profusely and made her way out of the building. On the long walk home, Emma wondered how she was going to tell Jake about this, and more so, how she could persuade him to let her follow through with it.

Baby Travis had been in bed for some time when Jake finally walked in the door. As he smelled of alcohol, Emma figured he had stopped for a few beers with his buddies on his way home from work.

"Jake, there's something I'd like to talk to you about," Emma began. "Can you sit and listen for a bit?"

Jake sat down at the kitchen table. "Yeah, what is it?"

Emma began telling him about going for a walk with Travis and spotting the sign for daycare help. She thought it would be healthy for Travis to spend time around other kids, and it would bring some extra money into the household. Surprisingly, Jake agreed to it. The only problem was how to get Emma to the daycare center with one vehicle in the household.

They decided that Jake would drop Emma and Travis off at the Easy Stop as he headed off to work in the morning. Emma would walk the rest of the way into town with Travis. With spring nearly here, Emma thought their plan would work. She would worry about transportation home later.

The following Monday morning, Jake dropped Emma and Travis off at 7:30 as he continued on to work. Emma made it into town by 8:00. She and Travis entered the daycare center to a lively group of little ones. They ranged in age from toddlers to nearly five years old. Travis was delighted to be with the other children, and Emma found herself engaged with the various personalities.

The day passed quickly between outdoor activities, snacks, and naps. Emma breathed a sigh of relief when 5:00 rolled around, as she felt a bit weary, and Travis was already fast asleep in the corner. Another woman named Cheryl offered to drop Emma and Travis off at their house. Emma was most grateful.

"Cheryl, thank you so much! Can I pay you?"

Cheryl laughed. "Of course not. It's so nice to have another body to help out with all the kids."

This daily routine turned into a weekly, then monthly routine. Surprisingly, Jake willingly dropped Emma and Travis off each morning on his way to work. Travis blossomed being around the other children, and Emma found herself becoming attached to some of the little ones as well.

One evening upon arriving home after an extra busy day, Jake greeted Emma and Travis at the door. "Hey Emma, we need to talk," began Jake. "My boss is opening another store near Chico, and he wants me to manage it. It means more money and a raise for me."

Emma stopped in her tracks. Moving? She finally felt like she belonged somewhere and had made connections. "Jake, this is kind of sudden. Maybe we should talk about it."

"No, it's already decided. We're leaving at the end of the month, so let the daycare center know."

Emma felt deflated. She silently fed Travis and got him ready for bed. So much had happened. How could she continue to go on without the network of caring souls that had sprung up?

The following day, Emma entered the daycare center with a heavy heart. She found Kris and let her know of the impending move. Kris gave Emma a hug. "Emma, you will be fine. There will be other jobs for you. You are a special person with a big heart—that is so evident. Use me for a reference if you'd like."

Emma nodded. Inside, she didn't share Kris's optimism.

Jake, Emma, and Travis settled in Paradise, a small community in the foothills. Emma loved the trees and the serenity that seemed to surround her. Jake continued to occupy himself with his job. Emma decided that she would not be a prisoner in her own home. As hard as it might seem, she would reach out and meet others. She had learned previously how important that emotional support was to her well-being and to Travis's, too.

Emma began taking Travis out for walks. She met other young mothers with little ones. Before Emma knew it, she became connected with another daycare center and was working once again. Even though her life with Jake was lacking in intimacy or any real affection, Emma felt fulfilled working with the other women and children.

One summer day, Josie, another worker at the center, mentioned that she was going to start taking early childhood education classes at Butte College, a local community college. "Emma, you should really consider it. Having a degree will enable you to earn more at a larger daycare center."

"I don't know ... Jake would never agree to my going to school, especially with Travis."

"Well, think about it. It will definitely help you in getting future jobs."

Emma did think about it. She went to the library and pored over the Butte College website and the requirements for an early childhood education degree. "I can do this," she told herself. Emma felt drawn to early childhood education. It seemed only natural after having a child of her own and working at the different daycare centers.

Surprisingly, Jake agreed to Emma taking classes and pursuing a degree in education. He decided to attend Butte as well. Jake did insist that he and Emma take at least one class together. He said it would be helpful for them to study with one another, and it would save on commuting and babysitting costs. While Emma had her doubts, she was elated that Jake had agreed to this.

Classes for the fall semester began two weeks later. Emma and Jake shared an English class. Jake appeared to be in his element surrounded by so many attractive women. Emma tried to ignore Jake's endless flirtations with the ladies and instead focus on her studies.

While it hurt Emma to view Jake treating others the way he once treated her, Emma consoled herself with the thought that college was a good thing. She was a better parent for Travis, and if she ever needed to support herself, well…

The classes at Butte College continued until Emma had the necessary units to transfer to Chico State University. Emma decided upon pursuing a bachelor's degree in education. With the great love Emma had for children, she felt that this was a natural fit.

Chico State University was all Emma thought it would be and more. She found the classes challenging and awakening new desires deep within her. She enjoyed being around other students and hearing the variety of discourse that is so often found in a college setting.

It wasn't easy being a mom, student, and trying to work a few hours at the daycare center to cover expenses. Then there was Jake. While he was taking classes as well, he seemed to be home less and less. There were frequent excuses—study hours with other students, writing papers in the library, and so on. After a while, Emma didn't seem to mind. It was evident that they were drifting apart and each was pursuing a different path.

The final straw came one night when Jake wandered in past midnight. Emma met him at the door. "Jake, I've been worried. Where have you been? Travis missed you."

A mixture of alcohol and a woman's fragrance drifted her way. "I told you—I had studying to do," he snarled.

Noticing some lipstick on his face, she replied, "Yeah, I can see that."

Emma knew what had to be done for both Travis and her. How she would manage financially she wasn't sure, but she had to try.

The next day while on campus, Emma visited the student services office and inquired about the legal services they offered. She spoke with a clerk named Carol. Carol assured Emma that help was available for those seeking either a legal separation or dissolution of marriage.

She let out a sigh of relief. "Thank you."

Emma left with a stack of paperwork to complete before any appointment could be scheduled. Next on her agenda was to look for some type of affordable housing in town. How could she manage anything while a student and working a few hours a week? The answer came with Emma's friend, Tiffany, who offered Emma a room in her home.

Moving in with Tiffany made things a bit crowded, but Emma knew that was the only way she could afford college and living on her own. Jake had already balked at the amount of support proposed by Emma's attorney. Emma filled out countless forms for student aid and anything else she could find, telling herself that this was as much for Travis as for herself.

The days were full between classes, working at the daycare center, and spending time with Travis. Her young son would soon be two years old. He was growing and changing into a little man daily before Emma's eyes, and she was so proud of him. While Emma had to share custody of Travis with Jake, she used the time away from him to focus on her studies and work at the daycare center. One night after a wearying day of work and classes, her friend Cassie suggested that Emma join her for coffee and studying. Emma at first offered an excuse, then changed her mind saying, "That sounds great, Cassie. I could really use someone to study with."

Cassie and Emma found a small table in the corner of the crowded coffee bar. It seemed that others had the same idea about cramming for tests. Emma was enjoying having no responsibility other than reviewing notes for class the next day.

"Hey, Cassie—what's up?" asked a tall, blond-haired guy.

"Hi, Mattie. Nothing. We're just catching up on some studying.

Oh, this is Emma," Cassie said, gesturing in her direction.

Emma looked up. "Hi."

"Hi," he replied.

Emma noticed that his eyes twinkled whenever he spoke, as though he was concealing a secret he couldn't wait to blurt out.

They chatted briefly, then Mattie moved on. "He seems nice," Emma commented.

"Yeah, he is," replied Cassie.

Studies resumed, and Emma forgot about Mattie. A week later, Emma and Cassie were once again studying in their favorite coffee bar.

"Hi," said a voice.

They both looked up to see Mattie's grin. "Hey, you want to join us?" asked Cassie.

"Sure," he replied.

Between work and classes, Emma scarcely had time to breathe. It felt odd how Emma seemed to run into Mattie wherever she went; it might be in Aroma Coffee, student services, crossing campus, or elsewhere. One afternoon while poring over notes before heading to class, Emma sensed someone nearby and looked up. Standing to her left was Mattie with a broad smile plastered on his face. "You look like you're studying pretty intensely. Must be a big test."

"Yeah, between work and my son, Travis, it's hard to find enough time for studying."

"Maybe it's something I can help you with. What class is it?"

"U.S. History."

"Hey, that's one of my favorites. History is my major. Let me see what you're reviewing," Mattie enthused while reaching for Emma's book.

She laughed. "I guess it's my lucky day!"

"I guess so," he replied with a sparkle in his eyes.

Emma started spending more and more time with Mattie. He even came to the tiny apartment she now shared with Travis. The two seemed to really hit it off. Mattie was so patient with him. There were piggyback rides, tumbling on the floor, and Mattie's favorite indulgence for Travis when Emma wasn't looking: Klondike bars. The two of them would sit side-by-side on the couch, enjoying their Klondike bars while the ice cream dribbled down their chins. As soon as Emma entered the room, Mattie would hide them behind his back; ice cream was a kitchen thing, Emma had said. This caused endless peals of laughter from Travis, as he thought they were getting away with something big. Emma would simply smile, so grateful for the love and attention that Travis was receiving.

The days passed quickly. While Mattie had already finished his bachelor's degree, he continued to take classes toward a master's while holding down a part-time job. Emma had decided to pursue teaching rather than early childhood education. She felt that she would have more impact on the lives of older kids. Mattie looked at her with such affection, stating, "I'm behind you, whatever you decide to do."

Emma found it challenging juggling classes, working, and sharing Travis with her ex-husband. Jake quickly remarried and demanded that Travis spend more time with him and his new wife, Holly. Emma anguished over how she could surrender her child to a man who had been unreliable at best. Somehow Mattie was there to both encourage and console her during those low points.

"You are a great mother. Travis is so lucky to have you. No one can change that," Mattie enthused while taking her in his arms.

"Besides, someone once told me that life is like putting a jigsaw puzzle together. We focus on a certain part of the puzzle, searching for pieces we think we need, frantic when we can't find them. But, God sees the picture on the box. He knows what the finished image will look like. We have to trust things to Him while we are searching for that next piece or whatever we think it is."

Emma smiled back. She wondered how she had been so lucky to meet this man. He treated her with dignity and respect, besides showing immense kindness toward her young son. Yes, she was blessed indeed.

The seemingly endless days of classes, work, and motherhood finally drew to an end for Emma. Graduation was days away. Emma reflected on the past few years and all that had taken place: There was the marriage to Jake that ended so painfully.

The only good thing that had come of that was Travis, who would soon be five years old.

Emma once again possessed a sense of self-worth thanks to an amazing man who had encouraged and challenged her along the way. Getting her degree came as a direct result of his influence in her life. She now felt such hope and joy as to what the future might hold for her.

Someone was indeed looking out for her and blessing her at the same time.

That day, Emma's phone buzzed; looking down, she saw it was Mattie. "Hi, I was just thinking of you."

"Well I was thinking of you and Travis as well. How about if we head out for a walk then stop for some ice cream afterwards? Do you think Travis would be up for that?"

"Are you kidding? You needn't ask—of course he will be!"

"Great. I'll be over in 15 minutes."

⇒⇒⇒⇒ ⇐⇐⇐⇐

Gina sat transfixed as Emma finished her story. "I didn't know any of that. Mattie never mentioned a word to me as to how the two of you met or all that you've gone through."

"He wouldn't." Emma looked up with tears in her eyes. "That's the type of man he was. I miss him so much."

"I know. We all do," Gina said as tears welled up in her own eyes.

As the women left the restaurant, Gina pondered what she had learned about her son tonight. While she thought Mattie was an amazing man, he was her son after all. She never had a clue as to the influence Mattie had exerted on Emma's life.

The ladies walked down the street to the downtown parking lot. Gina put her arms around Emma for a hug. "Emma, call me if you need anything or want to talk."

"I will. You do the same."

While they had been together for just a few hours, it seemed as though days had passed. Gina felt a weariness descend upon her.

"Abby, I'm exhausted. How about heading back to our room?"

"I feel the same way. It's been some day."

Chapter 5

After breakfast the following morning, Gina said, "I'd really like to spend some time downtown. I want to visit the spots Mattie and I used to frequent. Do you mind?"

"Of course not! Take all the time you need. I'll call Emma to see how she's doing today."

Walking down Second Street, every shop or building seemed to remind Gina of the many weekends she had spent in Chico over the years. Of course, the object of her visits was to hang out with her son.

How do I move forward from this emptiness I feel? She wondered. *Everywhere I look I see images of him.*

Mattie had always seemed to know where to take Gina when she visited, whether it was for lunch, an espresso, or a community event. How much fun they had last July when they roamed the streets of the city experiencing a "Slice of Chico." The sidewalks were lined with merchants showcasing their goods for sale. The sun baked down on them as they wandered the streets. Just when Gina felt that she couldn't take another step, a tub filled with ice-cold watermelon greetedher. Biting into the sweet fruit brought relief and encouraged her on. Gina remembered the raucous laughter surrounding the children andthe watermelon roll; some of the watermelons were nearly as large as the kids themselves.

Gina ducked under a large fir on the Chico campus for relief from the heat that was gradually building. Mattie's presence seemed to inhabit the area. She could see him striding across campus with his long gait and radiant smile. Always a smile on his face, no matter what life brought his way.

Continuing to wander the walkways, Gina felt Mattie by her side, guiding her to various sights as he had done on so many occasions. "Mom, you have to see Bidwell Mansion. People come from all over to see it decked out at Christmas." Or, "You don't want to miss the farmer's market and their beef jerky." Of course he would also point out the stately old buildings gracing the downtown area, along with a brief history lesson.

She could almost hear, "Hey Mom, how about grabbing a burger?" Or, "We could go to Tres Hombres for lunch."

Invariably Mattie would encounter others he knew as they strolled the streets. There would always be a grin and "How are you doing, man?"

She missed him and that smile. He always seemed to be smiling with the corners of his eyes crinkled in delight. No matter what might be happening in his life, he always exuded warmth and caring towards others.

Gina headed to one of their favorite hangouts—Aroma Coffee. As she walked in, she was assaulted by the rich smell of coffee beans. A variety of croissants and muffins greeted her in the display case. She ordered a latte, then moved toward the back room, wanting to be alone with her thoughts. Quietness enveloped the coffee shop. The morning regulars must have already retrieved their daily fix, then left before the heat of the day descended upon them.

Gina spotted a worn velvet love seat in the corner, the perfect location for a bit of solitude. She took out her iPhone and began scrolling through photographs of Mattie. One in particular caught her eye: Mattie in his graduation gown, a wide grin plastered across his face. How she remembered that day. He had been so exuberant and was ready to take on the world.

"My plan is to work one year, then begin a graduate program in history. I may continue on with a Ph.D."

"Whoa, slow down, Mattie!" Gina admonished. "Give yourself some time to decompress and enjoy life a bit."

"I will, Mom. I can do both," he stated with confidence.

He never did slacken his pace. True to his word, he worked for one year then began grad school. How proud she was of him.

Tears slid down Gina's face. Lost in thought, Gina didn't notice the young man who had come into the back room. He sat down at the table next to her. Feeling eyes upon her, Gina looked up, meeting the stranger's gaze. Something about him seemed vaguely familiar. Maybe it was the faded jeans and UC Chico t-shirt like the ones Mattie used to wear.

He smiled at her.

She looked away, focusing instead on the heart-shaped foam in her latte.

"Having a rough day?"

Gina hadn't planned on discussing with anyone the utter despair that consumed her, or how she wished she were the one in Larson's Funeral Home instead of her son. After all, it should have been her; children aren't supposed to die before their parents. "You might say that."

The stranger motioned toward Gina's phone and the picture of Mattie in cap and gown. "A recent grad?"

"No, it's been a while. Just recalling a special memory."

"Ah, yes. There are many of those in life."

Gina took a sip of her coffee, and the stranger did likewise. Feeling a bit awkward that her privacy had been invaded, Gina wanted to leave before any more conversation ensued.

The young man looked up with a smile. "I'm Bart," he said, extending his hand to Gina.

While not wanting to engage Bart further in conversation, she returned the greeting with, "I'm Gina."

Putting her iPhone in her purse, Gina started to rise.

"Gina, please wait. We should talk. I know why you're here."

Gina's face registered complete astonishment. "What are you talking about?" she demanded. "I think you have me mistaken with someone else. I don't even know you." She had had enough; it was time to return to the hotel and Abby.

"Your only son. You're angry that he was snatched away from you at such a young age, aren't you?" Bart prodded.

Gina's gray eyes flashed. "How do you know that? What do you know about the drunk driver who killed my son? I hope he rots in hell!"

"I have *connections*, you might say."

Gina studied the young man again. Ash-brown hair, blue eyes, medium build, nothing out of the ordinary, yet there was something about him that registered in the back of her mind.

"Have we met before?" she asked suspiciously.

He laughed. "I have one of those familiar-looking faces. I'm convinced that each of us has a twin somewhere out there."

Pulling out his iPhone, he asked, "Maybe you'd like to see this—the impact of your son's life?"

Gina gave Bart a bewildered look. "I don't know what you're talking about. Did you know my son?"

"Gina just watch. Mattie made a difference. You gotta believe that.

Bart clicked on a video, and Mattie suddenly appeared on the screen.

Gina watched as the video unfolded. It was the first semester of his freshman year at Chico State University when Mattie met Kellie. She walked into his political science class. She had a beaming smile, and long, blond hair framed a heart-shaped face. Mattie couldn't keep his eyes off her. When class ended, he walked by her, smiled, and said, "Hi."

"Hi," she returned somewhat shyly. "Where are you heading?"

"I have a break before my next class begins. I thought I'd grab a cup."

"Do you want some company?"

"Sure; that would be great," Kellie replied, smiling at him.

That coffee led to others along with many dates. Kellie became an important part of Mattie's life. They were dating exclusively.

As the video continued, Gina gasped as she saw herself on the screen. It had been several years earlier while Mattie was a mere eighteen-year-old. Gina had just picked up her ringing phone. The caller was Mattie. "Hi honey," she said. "How are things going?"

"Fine, Mom. Hey, do you mind if I bring Kellie home for Christmas?"

"Of course not. It would be great to have her join us. Just forewarn her that we have a few quirks in our family," laughed Gina.

"Will do," he replied.

Gina interrupted the video with an accusatory tone. "I don't know who you work for or how you obtained these videos, but it's none of your business. These are private moments." Her eyes flashed in anger.

"Gina, my boss has access to all sorts of information. *He* wants you to view these for a reason. Please, indulge me a bit further." With that, Bart once again resumed the video where he had paused it before Gina's outburst.

Christmas was extra special having Kellie there. She seemed to fit right in. Gina and Kellie hit it off with their talk about clothes, sewing and other topics. Kellie was debating pursuing a degree in design or communications. She had been designing and making many of her own clothes for some time.

"What do you hope to do with either degree?" Gina inquired. "Well, with design I could potentially land a job with a firm in San Francisco. I could learn so much working under experienced designers. Eventually I'd like to design my own line of clothing."

"That sounds wonderful. You certainly have talent!" Gina enthused after seeing some of Kellie's work.

"There's a study abroad program in the spring that I've signed up for. It's based in Paris, but travel to Milan and Rome is included with it."

The rest of the evening didn't seem so long with Kellie there. Mattie felt exasperated when his Uncle Ted went on and on about politics. Of course, this led to many arguments between Uncle Ted and his sister, Vicki, who held different political views. For once it would be nice not to have to listen to the countless debates. Mattie helped his mom pass out champagne. They raised their glasses to toast to the blessings of family, the past year, and the year to come. It truly was a wonderful Christmas.

Gina looked up. "I remember that so vividly. It was such a lovely day!" Her face darkened, "But then Kellie broke Mattie's heart."

"That she did."

"Mattie cared for her so much. He should have realized that Kellie's affections would wander while she traveled in Europe."

Bart picked up his phone to resume the video when Gina reached for his hand, preventing him from doing so. "I want a few answers. Are you C.I.A.? Have you been spying on my son and our family?"

Bart looked at her with an amused smile, his eyes crinkling in delight. Those eyes were so familiar to her. Where had she seen them before?

"No, Gina, I'm not with the C.I.A. or any other *earthly* organization. Please let me continue; I assure you everything will become clear soon enough."

Gina sighed, "Fine. I'll give you five more minutes, then I'm leaving." She looked down at the phone as the video once again resumed playing.

In the video, the end of January arrived, and with it, Kellie leaving for her study abroad program. Mattie told himself that May would arrive before he knew it, and they would be together once again. Mattie joined Kellie's parents at San Francisco airport to send her on her way.

At the security checkpoint, they said their farewells. "I'll call or text every day—I promise," Kellie said as Mattie hugged her goodbye.

"I will, too."

Mattie made what seemed like an endless drive back to Chico, feeling empty and alone inside. He would focus on school, work, and somehow he would get through the next few months.

Kellie and Mattie continued to talk or text daily. On one particular day he received a frantic text from her: *Matt, I really need your help. I have a paper due in my history class. I've been so busy with my design projects I haven't been able to work on it much. If I email it to you, can you help me with it? Please?*

Of course Mattie promised he would do so. He called Gina the following day. "Hey Mom, can I ask you for some help?"

"Sure, honey, what's up?"

Mattie recounted the frantic text from Kellie, then continued, "Mom, what she wrote is terrible. I know this paper counts for a big chunk of her grade. Would you mind looking at it as well and making a few changes? You used to do the same thing for me."

"Of course. I'll make adjustments and highlight those for you."

"Thanks, Mom. I love you."

"Love you as well."

Gina opened her email and began poring over the paper. She sighed as she read the text. Mattie wasn't kidding; it was terrible. While Kellie had much talent in design, her writing lacked even fundamental skills. After rewriting and editing for several hours, Gina emailed Mattie: *Hi honey, these are the changes I made. I spent four hours on this, and it needs much more. I can't commit to any more time in helping Kellie. You should do the same. I know you care about Kellie and want to see her do well in her class, but she needs to accept responsibility for her own work.*

Mattie continued helping with the paper for several more days, even though his calls and texts to Kellie were left unanswered.

Finally, Kellie called one day. "Hi Matt. I wanted to let you know that I've met someone else here. We've been going out for a while.

Maybe you should do the same instead of waiting for me." Then Kellie hung up.

Mattie listened, shell-shocked. The last eight weeks had been long ones. He had been counting the days until Kellie returned. Now this. He called Gina and poured out his heart.

"I'm so sorry, Matt." Her heart ached for her son. What could she say to ease his pain? She too, knew the feeling of betrayal from her relationship with Bryan. How Gina wished she could have spared him from this heartache, but she knew that pain is an inevitable part of life. "Something positive will come from this at a later point in time. You have to believe that."

"Will do, Mom," and he hung up the phone.

Gina looked up with tears in her eyes, remembering that incident so clearly. *Why would Bart's boss want her to relive that painful memory in light of her own recent loss?*

"What did you tell Mattie after Kellie broke his heart? Remember, he had spent all that time helping her with her paper and she had used him?" Bart asked.

"You showed Kellie unmerited kindness. No one can ever take that away from you."

"Yes, but what else?" prodded Bart.

"You gave Kellie a precious gift with your help. While it may appear that the giftee reaps all the benefits, in truth, the giver receives more," Gina replied softly.

"And why is that?"

"It's a heart issue." Gina looked Bart in the eyes. *He wasn't a college student; she could sense that. But who was he?* She wondered.

"Isn't that where most problems begin—in the heart?"

"I suppose. Bart, why don't you explain to me who you really are and why you are here. You are not a college student; that's clear to me," Gina demanded a bit abruptly. She looked at Bart in his Chico State shirt and the light stubble on his chin, wondering how he would know any of this or have access to such private information.

Bart shifted a bit in his chair, taking another sip of his coffee.

"I don't understand how you got ahold of these videos. There's no possible way," Gina stated.

"You're right. There is *no way*. As I said, I do have *connections*." Gina stared intently at the stranger. "I'm not sure I understand."

"I've been sent here to let you know that Mattie made a difference. His life mattered. Many times, those on earth never realize the impact their lives have on others until they depart this world, and they're on the other *side.*"

"The other side … You mean you are from…?" Gina didn't finish, as the realization of what Bart was saying finally hit her. She looked at him with a quizzical look. "You're an angel?"

He nodded his head.

"I've been under a lot of stress lately. This is not reallyhappening. I need to talk to someone to help me deal with the loss of my son."

"Gina, you're not imagining anything. I was sent here for a reason.

He knows your pain."

Tears began streaming down Gina's face once more. If Bart was an angel, then *He* had to be...

"If the Lord above knows the number of hairs on your head or the grains of sand on a beach, don't you think He is aware of the burden you are carrying? Let *Him* carry it for you."

Bart picked up his phone. "You need to see this. Yes, love involves risk and potential hurt," he commented. "In spite of all that, it makes us more aware of others and their needs. Let me show you what I mean." He gestured toward his phone as another video appeared.

Kellie had a roommate named Natalie. Mattie would often encounter Natalie at Kellie's apartment, or when he and Kellie were out and about on campus. One Thursday afternoon as Mattie was waiting for Kellie, Natalie arrived home with what looked like a black eye. Mattie studied the girl, then asked, "Natalie, are you okay?"

"Yeah, fine," she said, ducking inside her room.

Later, Mattie questioned Kellie about it. "Hey, what happened to Natalie? It looked like someone laid into her."

Kellie stared at Mattie somberly. "That's exactly what happened. Natalie had a disagreement with Jesse. That's how he settled it." Mattie was enraged. "He can't do that! Let me at him!"

"No, Mattie. That would make things worse. You need to let Natalie decide what to do."

A few days later, Jesse showed up at the apartment while Mattie happened to be there. "Is Natalie around?" Jesse slurred.

Walking up to him, Mattie stated, "Natalie is a friend of mine, and I don't like what I've been seeing. If Natalie shows up with any more bruises, you and I are going to have a problem. Understand?"

Jesse glared at Mattie and stalked off.

"Natalie, you're too good for him," declared Mattie. "You need to end things. There are so many guys who would give anything to be with you. Let him go."

"I don't know … You don't know Jesse like I do. He's a good guy."

"Natalie, listen to me. Guys like that don't change," insisted Mattie. "If he ever touches you again, there's no telling what I'll do to him. Walk away while you can."

A week later, Natalie arrived home with bruises covering her face and left arm. Mattie and Kellie accompanied Natalie downtown to press assault and battery charges against Jesse.

"Natalie, please end this now before something worse happens," pleaded Mattie.

"I will. Promise," said Natalie with tears streaming down her face.

"Mattie never mentioned anything about Kellie's roommate or her situation." Gina leaned back in the love seat, shaking her head slightly. "That poor girl. Guys like that should be locked up. Why do women get involved with such jerks?" She thought back to her own dysfunctional relationship with Bryan.

What else was there about her son that she was unaware of?

Chapter 6

art continued on without giving her a moment to process the previous information. "Gina, think back over the years. Did you ever wonder if things were more than just coincidences? That you just happened to be in a particular location at just the right time? Remember when Mattie was little and the two of you were flying through Dallas-Ft. Worth on your way to Missouri? Do you remember the gentleman in the restaurant? That meeting occurred for a reason; it was preordained. If you hadn't been there things would have turned out very differently."

Gina searched her memory.

Gina and Mattie were at the Dallas-Ft. Worth Airport awaiting a connecting flight to Kansas City. Gina thought it important that her young son meet some of her family, especially since Mattie didn't have a relationship with his dad.

"Come on Mattie, you need to stay with Mommy," Gina urged as the toddler ran off giggling.

Mattie ran up to a table in the food court where a lone businessman sat eating. The boy toddled up to the stranger with a huge smile on his face.

The businessman, Rob, had been traveling on a trip that routed him through Dallas-Ft. Worth. He had been struggling the past few weeks with many things—his marriage, his job, and the demands of life itself. Glancing at the departure board, he noted that his American Airlines flight was running behind schedule.

"Late again. What a surprise!" he muttered.

Spying a Five Guys hamburger joint, he thought a burger would help fill his time. While munching on his burger and fries, he noticed a young mom with a very active toddler nearby. The little one headed straight for his table with the biggest smile Rob had seen in some time. The boy stopped in front of him with his gaze fixed on Rob.

"Hi, guy," said Rob. "Do you want some of these?" he extended his hand with a few fries.

The stranger had just shoved a handful of French fries into his own mouth. Mattie lingered, gazing at both the man and the fries, smiling all the while.

"Here, have some," the stranger said again, extending his hand.

Mattie grabbed them and tried to put them into his mouth. All the while he kept smiling at the man as the fries fell on the floor.

Gina rushed over. "I'm sorry," she stammered. "He's usually not this intrusive."

"No problem. I'm sort of enjoying the company," replied the stranger with a smile.

"Thank you for your patience," Gina said as she led the small boy away. Rob gazed after them as the mom and her son left the food court. He remembered when life had been more like that for him and his wife, Angie. Rob missed those days. Lately it seemed that all they did was argue. Where had their love and family relationship gone? Inwardly he resolved to try and recover what they once had. That little boy stirred something inside him he hadn't felt for some time.

Gina questioned Bart, "You said that 'if Mattie and I hadn't been there, things would have turned out much differently for Rob. What do you mean?"

"Let me show you." And with that, Bart tapped on his phone yet again. Another video appeared. "Here you go," he said, handing the phone to Gina.

Back in the airport Rob glanced at the departure board. No surprise, his flight to Des Moines was delayed, as usual. He spied a bar nearby. A drink or two would help. Life had been more than he could handle lately. His wife, Angie, was always complaining about something. It seemed that he could do nothing right. Work was not much better. Sales were down, and his new boss was expecting him to clinch the account in Des Moines.

Rob slid into a seat at the bar. A cute server came up to him and asked what he'd like. He glanced at the beer selection momentarily, then thought, what the heck, why order beer? "Scotch and soda," he replied.

"Sure thing, darling," she drawled back. He took a second look at her and liked what he saw. Long, dark hair pulled back in a ponytail, a face around late-30s, and her shapely body was more appealing than Angie's.

That one drink led to several. Before Rob knew it, he was becoming quite friendly with the server, Julie. Rob made plans to meet Julie when her shift ended. He decided that he could take a later flight to Des Moines. He'd sleep on the plane and make his pitch the following day. Besides, it had been a while since Angie had offered affection of any sort. Rob felt he was justified in this small dalliance. After all, it was only one night.

Rob and Julie hit a couple of bars playing country and western music. They laughed, danced, drank, and did more of the above. Before he realized what was happening, they ended up in her apartment, and one thing led to another.

The next morning, Rob woke with a start. His head throbbed. Rubbing it, he was trying to remember what had happened. He saw the brunette with the tousled hair in bed next to him, then remembered the night before. He glanced at the clock nearby and groaned. 7:20. He had already missed his 7:00 flight to Des Moines, and his presentation was only two and a half hours away. He swore silently to himself as he jumped out of bed, fumbling for his clothes.

Rob made it to the airport by 8:15. The next flight to Des Moines was at 10:20. He groaned inside. Damage control was what was needed now.

Rob picked up his cell phone and called his home office. "Hey, Larry, it's Rob. You won't believe what happened. I got some food poisoning while waiting for my connection last night. Yeah, I took something to help and just slept all night. Needless to say, I missed my earlier flight. Can you call Ericson in Des Moines and do some damage control? Man, I'll be eternally grateful. Thanks," he sighed as he hung up.

What was he thinking? He only hoped that he didn't lose either the account or his job. He didn't want to think of how he'd look at Angie, knowing that he had cheated on her.

"As you can see, *He* had you and Mattie in that fast-food restaurant for a reason. *He* knows the hearts and needs of those committed to Him."

Gina looked up with tears in her eyes. "I never really thought about how one decision could alter the course of one's life so dramatically. I doubt Rob thought about it, either. Would things have worked out for him?"

Bart slowly shook his head. "No."

"Mattie was like that. He loved people and always wanted to be surrounded by them. That's just my point—why did he have to die? Why wasn't it me instead? I've lived a full life. I've been able to travel and do so much, why not me? It wasn't right for him to be taken at such a young age. Then there's that drunk driver—what I would like to see happen to him!"

Bart sat there listening intently, occasionally nodding his head to indicate that he understood.

Gina continued ranting until exhaustion seemed to overtake her. Burying her head in her hands, she wept. "I can't do this. It's too much for me." Her chest felt like it was closing in, and breathing was beginning to come in short gasps. She struggled not to succumb to panic.

Bart watched as Gina let out all her pent-up emotion. She remained like that for several minutes. "You will see better days. I promise," he assured her.

Chapter 7

*G*ina stared blankly into her empty cup. So much had happened in the past few days which she was struggling to make sense of. Her son dying unexpectedly, Emma's story of Mattie's impact on her life, and now this stranger implying that he was not of this world and showing her things that might have been.

"Bart, this is more than I can handle right now. I really need to go." Gina started to rise.

"Gina, I was sent here for a reason. As I said, *He* knows what you're going through. He is aware of every tear you have shed, and they are precious to Him; so precious that He collected each one in a bottle with your name on it. There are no coincidences. There is a purpose for each situation in one's life. If you don't believe that, let me show you." Bart scrolled through his cell phone once more.

"Bart, please, I've had enough of your videos and your 'what-if' scenarios."

Bart gazed at Gina earnestly. Where had she seen that look before? "Please indulge me one more time—please?"

Another video appeared on his phone.

In the video, Mattie was walking with his friend, Jason, to Jason's house. Jason opened the door tentatively. "Mom, are you here?"

Both boys walked into the darkened living room. Jason's mom sat slumped over in a chair. Jason walked over and nudged her gently. "Mom, Mom, wake up. Are you okay?"

On the table sat an empty bottle of pills along with something that looked like alcohol. Jason picked up the glass and took a whiff. "Uggh," he said setting it down again. He picked up the bottle and read the prescription: OxyContin.

"Mom used this for pain after she hurt her back. You don't think...?"

Mrs. Olson's eyes flickered a bit, then closed.

Jason was becoming more frantic. "Mom, come on. Wake up!" Jason looked over at Mattie desperately. "What should I do?"

"Does she have a pulse?"

Jason grabbed her wrist. "I feel something, but it's weak."

"Call 911!"

Jason picked up the phone and made the call. Minutes later, a fire truck roared up. A paramedic rushed in and set to work on Mrs. Olson.

"Son, we need to take her to the hospital."

Jason gulped. "Okay."

"You can ride with us unless there is someone else who can drive you," stated the paramedic.

"Jason, I'll ask Mom if she'll give us a ride."

"That would be great! Sir, I'll go with my friend."

"Sure thing, son."

Mattie called his mom and briefly filled her in on the happenings. "I'll be right over," she said.

Mattie and Jason were waiting outside as Gina pulled up in her Chevy Tahoe. Gina rushed out and gave Jason a hug. "Jason, she'll be okay. You have to believe that."

"Yeah, Ms. Martin."

"Mom, let's pray for Jason's mom right now."

Mattie, Jason, and Gina bowed their heads and sent up fervent pleas to the God who hears and sees all.

"Come on," said Gina, wiping away a tear. "Let's go see your mom."

The trio pulled up to the hospital and silently made their way inside. Mattie continued to plead with God. "Lord, please help her to be okay. Jason really needs a mom."

Checking in at the front desk, they learned which room Mrs. Olson was situated in. "Jason, would you like me to talk to the nurse for you?' asked Gina.

"Sure, Ms. Martin," he replied.

Gina approached a nurse and pulled her aside. She explained that Jason was her son's friend. As Jason was under the age of 18, could Gina speak on his behalf and take responsibility for him until another guardian could be located? The nurse considered the request, then replied, "I don't see why not."

As it turned out, Mrs. Olson had mixed alcohol with prescription drugs. She came close to overdosing. Jason and Mattie had intervened at just the right time. "Mattie, I don't know what would have happened if you and I hadn't walked in when we did."

"We were there for a reason," Mattie replied.

"Mrs. Olson lived as a result of the boys finding her in time," Bart said.

"I remember that."

"You probably aren't aware of the kind of childhood that Jason experienced. If his mom hadn't made it, his life would have had a much different outcome."

"I can only imagine."

"Can you, Gina? No dad in the picture. No immediate family. Raised by near strangers who don't really want you."

"I didn't know…"

"Jason is now working on a master's degree in counseling. He's in a program that helps those with substance abuse issues. That would not have happened if Mattie had not been with him on that fateful day."

Gina sat back in the chair, letting Bart's words sink in. Two lives which were forever altered. Altered in a positive way. "And Mrs. Olson, how is she?"

"She went through rehab and a counseling program. It was quite a journey dealing with all the demons inside her, but she is now doing well. Clean and sober. A believer, I might add."

"That is wonderful news. I'm so glad to hear that."

"Would you like to see how lives would have been impacted differently had Mattie never been born?"

Gina's head jerked up. "What do you mean, if 'he'd never been born?' What are you implying?"

"I know that you contemplated ending your pregnancy; you wondered about you and Bryan. It wouldn't have made any difference in your relationship with him."

"How would you know that? Bryan was angry. He felt that I was trying to trick him into something permanent, though I wasn't."

Without saying a word, Bart clicked on his iPhone and another video appeared. This time it showed a much younger version of her, but one that was scarcely recognizable.

In the video, the alarm buzzed, and Gina groaned as she looked at the time—5:30 a.m. She'd have to hustle it in the shower before facing the commute traffic of the day. There must be something more to life than this perpetual tedium. While grateful to have a teaching position, living in the Bay Area was expensive and at times lonely. She had little opportunity to meet single men with interests similar to her own.

Gina thought of Bryan. Things had not gone well once he learned of her pregnancy. He was convinced that it was a ploy to trap him into something more permanent. They argued endlessly, even after she had the abortion. A few weeks later, Bryan moved out and left Gina with a rent that she could hardly afford.

Looking in the bathroom mirror, Gina wondered where her once youthful appearance had gone. In place of a pretty face, she now saw dark circles and a tired expression. Strands of gray were interspersed with her auburn hair. Where was her joy? She sighed deeply as she turned the hot water on.

Her second graders would add some delight to her day once she arrived at school. She dreaded the bumper-to-bumper commute, but jobs paid more here in the Bay Area. While squeaking by each month, she couldn't afford to take a salary cut by moving to a less expensive area. Between her student loans, rent, and other expenses, she was managing—if nothing monumental like a car repair occurred.

In Aroma Coffee, Gina looked down at the table, a sigh emanating from deep within. "I always wondered about that. Somehow I think I knew we weren't meant to be."

"So you made the right decision, keeping the baby."

"Yes."

"You already know what would have happened with Rob at the airport. Let's look at Kellie's life. You were angry with her for causing

so much hurt for your son, but even Kellie would have suffered had Mattie never been born."

The iPhone came to life once more, with Kellie this time. Kellie had long dreamed of becoming a fashion designer. She often made her own clothes and created ones for her friends. In just a few weeks she would be living and studying in Paris. Donna and Rick dropped their daughter off at the airport. "Call me baby, as soon as you arrive," instructed her mom.

"Promise, Mom. Bye—I love you both!"

The first weeks in Paris were a blur of excitement, between classes and seeing new sights. Kellie found herself caught up in a whirlwind of activity, people, and exhilaration. Attending classes and the people part were easy to handle; finding time for the papers and the reading she still had to do for her classes back home was becoming harder each day.

"Hey Kellie, we're off for some music and drinks. You're going to join us, aren't you?" asked her roommate Monique.

"I can't. I have this history paper I have to get done. I've procrastinated too long as it is. It's due next week."

"Come on, Kellie, you can do it later. Some fun will be good for you!"

After much protesting, Kellie finally relented. What a great time she had with Monique, Rico, and Alex. Kellie was so glad that she had joined her friends.

Rico seemed to want more than just friendship. She spent part of each day with him while the history paper languished on her laptop. The night before the paper was due, Kellie hastily typed something and emailed it off to her professor back home.

A week later, Kellie received a grade with a note attached: D-. Her paper showed a lack of preparation or insight on the subject. If she hoped to pass the class, more effort was required.

Kellie consoled herself that it was only one paper; she could pull her grade up. Unfortunately, the call of Rico and other adventures beckoned a bit louder than that of history.

Kellie ended her semester abroad with the realization that she had failed history and would have to make up the class. How was she going to explain this to her parents? Would that mean a semester of summer school? After a lively semester abroad, the thought of spending summer in a small college town was less than appealing. Kellie boarded her flight back to the states a bit subdued.

Gina looked up. "Kellie deserved what she got. She chose having a good time over her schoolwork. I don't know if I have much sympathy for her."

Bart sighed. "Yes, Kellie did make her own choices. Nevertheless, this is merely a glimpse as to what her life *would* have been like had Mattie not been a part of it."

Bart scrolled through his phone and pulled up another image. This time it was of Emma. He handed Gina his phone without saying a word.

Gina let out a gasp as she looked at the lifeless eyes and disheveled appearance, nothing like the woman she knew. Emma paced back in forth in a small, drab room. Gina continued watching.

Emma picked up the crying baby. What had happened to her? She thought she had everything going for her while in high school: she was good looking, popular, smart, and had the love of her life, or so she thought. Here she was at nineteen with a baby and an abusive husband. While Jake was at work, she was stuck at home in the middle of nowhere without transportation or friends to support her.

"Shh," Emma murmured as Travis began to cry again. What could she do? Jake had ostracized Emma from her family and friends. She didn't have any money of her own. This was not life and not something she wanted for her small son, being a prisoner in her own home. She made a decision to leave, but how? Where could she go? Emma set the crying baby down and began to weep uncontrollably.

"Please stop. I can't bear to see any more heartache for Emma. She has been through so much already."

Bart put his phone aside and studied Gina.

Chapter 8

*G*ina looked Bart squarely in the eyes. "Bart, I can see that Mattie made a difference in many lives. I'm grateful that he did and so proud of him. Yet I'm still struggling to make sense of why he had to leave us when he did. Why couldn't he have been given a few more years?"

"His assignment was over, his job finished. It was time for him to return home."

"Job? What are you talking about? And home, what do you mean *home*? Mattie's home was with me and Emma!"

"He had a job to do. Each person has been bestowed—or gifted, if you will—with certain innate abilities. They are to use those gifts while on earth to make a difference in the lives of others."

"You showed me that Mattie *did* use his gifts," Gina insisted.

"Yes, he did. Others choose not to, or fight the gifting they have received. Mattie did not. He wore it proudly as a badge of honor. He finished his assignment early; it was time for him to receive his rewards, the ones that are promised to those who are faithful."

"But why *there?* Why not *here?* He could have been honored here in some way."

Bart let out a long sigh. "Gina, there's another home that's so much better than the one you know of here. No more pain, sickness, suffering, or tears. That's the home that Mattie is now experiencing."

"But what about his family?"

"He has plenty of family there—the family of believers. Mattie also has his grandparents, aunts, uncles, a half-sister—a child of Bryan's that you never knew about—and so many others. You know how Mattie loved to talk. Well, now he has many to converse with. There's Noah, King David, and others. Mattie is particularly interested in the challenges Noah faced while building the ark. And Jonah, can you imagine the stench that he was subjected to while in the whale's mouth? As you can see, Mattie has plenty of family and is much loved in his new home."

At a loss for words, Gina simply stared at Bart.

He continued, "Gina, Mattie's new home is beyond anything imaginable. Let your mind wander for a moment. You have seen much beauty here on earth in places like Yosemite, the Grand Canyon, and Glacier National Park. Now, try to envision a place where you have majestic, snow-capped mountains while at the same time the surf is breaking upon white sand beaches glistening with diamonds, not trash. Waterfalls cascade down cliffs while snow softly falls in a nearby pine forest. There is panoply of color with flowers you have never seen. Then there are the animals … You can't even begin to fathom the glorious sights before Mattie." Bart paused as if trying to find the right words.

"But…" Gina started to say.

"The sounds are beyond description: the heavenly host lift up their praises all day long in melodies that you might liken to stars singing their own worship tunes as they praise the Creator. You have to trust me about this when I say it's unfathomable in its grandeur. The splendor of heaven surpasses anything of loveliness you might view on Earth."

"But what about us left behind—Emma, Travis, and me? How do we go on without him?"

"You are a strong woman. Now your job is to be that support for Emma and Travis. Help them through the months to come. Let them lean on you. Mattie would want that. Remember, you are never alone. *He* is always with you. Pour out your sorrow, your fears, and cares to Him."

"I can try. Emma is struggling, I know."

"Besides, you have your *own* job to do."

"Bart, please, you keep speaking in riddles. What job do I have to do? I teach second graders. What else is expected of me?"

"Gina, you will figure that out. Think about your passions, what gets you moving each day. Those are gifts from *Him*; they are to be used to better the lives of others and this place *you* call *home*."

An audible sigh emanated from Gina's lips.

"I'm expecting that you will join him one day. Remember your last dinner together? You left Tres Hombres and watched Mattie cross the street to his car."

"I remember that well. It was the last time I ever saw him."

"When you see him again, it will be as though you parted mere seconds ago; 'Mom, I just finished dinner with you at Tres Hombres,' he will say as you enter Heaven's gates."

Remembrance of that last evening together with her son brought a smile to Gina's face. "I felt so much love for him, listening to him talk about his plans and watching the way his face lit up as he did so."

"Gina, for the believer, death is merely a pause, not the end. It's like putting a comma in a sentence rather than a period. A comma indicates there is more to come."

A lump formed in Gina's throat, and she blinked away tears as she listened to Bart's words.

Chapter 9

Bart glanced down at his iPhone. "My time is up. I have to go."

"Will I ever see you again?"

Smiling slightly, Bart shook his head no. He looked at Gina gently and said, "Gina, you have everything you need. Think back to those early years with Mattie and the truths you helped instill in him. Remember Awanas?"

A far-away look appeared on Gina's face. "I do. Mattie worked so hard to learn his verses and earn the Awana bucks that accompanied them."

"Yes, and what did he say?"

Gina thought back to that long-ago memory:

"Hey, Mom, are you ready to go?" asked Mattie as Gina rinsed the last of the dinner plates.

"Give me a minute, Mattie," she replied.

It was Tuesday night. Mattie always had Awanas on Tuesday night. Gina was so proud of her son as he memorized Bible verses and learned more about God. She hadn't been overly religious herself, but she had been learning through Mattie.

One of his friends from school, Dylan, attended Awanas and had invited Mattie. As Gina drove him to the church where Awanas was held, Mattie practiced the verse he had been working on for the week.

"I have loved thee with an everlasting love … Jeremiah 31.3," stated Mattie. "Mom, do you know that God has loved us with an everlasting love?" Mattie's face beamed as he asked this question.

Gina glanced over at her young son. Such love welled up inside her for him. Gina had been developing a relationship with her Heavenly Father as a result of Mattie and what he shared with her from Awana.

As Gina picked Mattie up later that night, she inquired how things went. Mattie remembered his verse and earned five more Awana bucks. He pulled out a Bible.

"Look Mom at what I bought. A Bible—a Bible for Dad. It can really change his life!" Mattie exclaimed.

Gina groaned inwardly. After several years of little interest, Bryan had decided that he did want to get to know his son. "Yes, Mattie, you are right," Gina replied. "But first your dad has to open it." She didn't feel too optimistic about that outcome occurring.

Gina looked at her son with love and admiration. Only seven years old, yet the compassion and insight he had for one so young was astounding. She tousled his blond hair and said, "I'm so proud of you and your hard work." He smiled back.

In the coffee shop, Gina gazed off as if seeing something from long ago. "I have loved you with an everlasting love. That was the last scripture he needed to earn the Bible."

"Keep that scripture close to your heart. Remember, *He* has loved you with an everlasting love. *His* love doesn't change regardless of what is happening all around you."

They rose from the table and headed toward the front door. During their conversation, several people had come in and were milling around the counter waiting to place coffee orders. Gina followed Bart outside into the heat of the day. She turned towards him, searching his face one last time. "Thank you for giving me a glimpse into my son's life and the difference he made in the lives of others. It has brought me some comfort."

"Mattie had an impact on more people than you'll ever know. Remember that."

"When you return—I mean, when you're in Heaven again—please give him a hug for me. Tell him I love him and miss him."

Bart looked at Gina with tenderness, then he flashed a smile she would know anywhere. "Will do."

With that, he crossed the street and was gone.

"Mattie!" Gina realized that she had just been given an hour with her son.

Chapter 10

*A*fter the realization hit Gina that she had spent an hour talking to her son, she remained frozen to the spot once Bart had vanished. Gina pinched herself a couple of times to ensure she was awake, that it had not been a dream. What a gift she had been given. She knew without a doubt that her son was doing well in his new home. Any mom would want that assurance. But more so, she had been given a glimpse into the future as well as the past. Mattie conveyed to her the magnificence of heaven and the impact his life had made on Earth.

Gina walked back to the hotel room with a quiet, reflective spirit about her. She decided not to share her experience at Aroma Coffee with the others. While Abby was her dearest, closest friend, Gina suspected that even Abby would feel that Gina had snapped. Grief will cause people to see or do things they normally wouldn't do. Poor Emma. She was in no shape to deal with anything else at this point.

"Hi," Gina called out as she entered the hotel room. "Have you spoken with Emma today?"

Abby looked at Gina curiously. There was something different about her, but Abby couldn't put her finger on it.

"I did. It sounds like she is trying to make it through the day one hour at a time. I told her that you would call her when you returned from downtown. How did it go?"

"While I was sort of dreading visiting many of the places Mattie and I used to frequent together, it ended up being fairly peaceful. I felt his presence all around me. It's almost like he's still here," Gina remarked with a slight smile.

Abby sensed a calm about her friend that hadn't been there earlier that morning. "I'm so glad. Somehow I suspect that Mattie will continue to look after you, even though he is no longer physically here."

"You're probably right. Emma needs that as well at this point. I'll give her a call."

While speaking to Emma on the phone, Gina clearly sensed brokenness in the young woman. Emma had been through so much with her failed marriage, being a single mom, returning to school, then meeting the love of her life, only to have her future hopes shattered into tiny pieces. Gina would continue to look after her; wasn't that what Mattie had suggested during their conversation?

The women met at the downtown Starbucks to discuss the memorial service that would be held for Mattie the following week. After Gina's earlier encounter with Mattie at Aroma

Coffee, she viewed that spot as sacrosanct and wanted it to remain hers alone.

They greeted each other with a warm embrace, then set to work planning the details of the service. "Emma, what do you think if Mattie is interred here in Chico? He loved this community, and somehow it seems fitting that he should remain here."

"That would be wonderful! Travis and I could visit him regularly. Travis misses him so much already."

"Would you mind checking what plots are available at Chico Cemetery? Abby, if you can help me plan the service, I'd appreciate it. Then between all of us, we can compile a list of those we need to notify of the date and time."

Abby and Emma eyed each other. What had happened with Gina, as she seemed somewhat different from yesterday? Calmer, more resolute as to what needed to be done.

The women set about their respective tasks. Gina called a former Awana leader and pastor friend who Mattie knew quite well. Pastor Mark agreed to say a few words at the service.

"Gina, I can say with utmost certainty that I know where Mattie is now. He loved God and his actions reflected that. He lived a life that was congruent in everyway."

"Thank you. I appreciate your kind words, and I feel the same."

"One more thing. If you don't mind my saying so, think about joining a grief support group when this is behind you. Grief is not a solitary journey, but one intended to be shared with others. Let me know whether you need any help locating a group."

"I will certainly do so. Thanks for the suggestion. I'll mention it to Emma as well."

Had Gina not had the encounter with Bart in Aroma Coffee, she probably would have ignored Pastor Mark's suggestion. Instead, she mulled it over and considered it wise counsel. She would even discuss it with Emma and suggest she consider it.

⊶≫≫⟩ ⟨≪≪⟨⊷

The ladies regrouped to share their progress. Emma reported that a small plot beneath a towering oak tree was available at Chico Cemetery.

"That sounds perfect. Mattie would feel right at home there."

Emma mentioned her conversation with Pastor Mark and his suggestion of joining a grief support group.

"That's probably a good idea, Gina. You will need someone to talk to in the months ahead, and while I'm always here for you, you might like another person's input."

'Thanks, Abby—I couldn't ask for a better friend than you," said Gina, giving her friend a grateful smile.

Emma agreed to look into what was available in Chico, as she knew she would continue to struggle with Mattie's absence in her life.

Then the task began of listing the various organizations that Mattie had been involved in. Gina was amazed as the list grew in length: humane society, Rotary Club, VIPS, campus aid, and so on. How was she unaware of the breadth of his community involvement?

She remembered visiting him one weekend while he volunteered at the humane society. Mattie seemed to glow as he showed her around the site. They started with the bunnies, made their way to the cats, and ended with the dogs. She mustered all the self-restraint she could find not to leave with a tan-and-white terrier named Willie. Her heart went out to all the dogs caged there, awaiting a forever home. Mattie's responsibilities included feeding the dogs, cleaning their cages, and just being a playmate to them. He excelled at the latter, as he loved playing.

Emma mentioned that Mattie served as a VIP—Volunteer in Police Service—during the weekly Thursday night markets. The summertime temperature in Chico often soared to 100-plus degrees. Mattie would ensure that folks attending the market stayed well hydrated, safe, and answered any questions posed to him.

"Yes, I remember Mattie describing his work as a VIP. He truly seemed to enjoy it," said Gina.

"He had a chance to be around the people he cared about. It was always about others with him. He was one of the most giving people I knew."

»»»» ««««

The day of the service arrived blazing hot, as Chico often times is in July. Chairs were set up under the shade of Valley Oak trees. An unadorned alabaster urn sat on a small table, surrounded by multicolored floral arrangements. Mattie lived a simple life. Gina wanted the ceremony to reflect that simplicity, along with the man Mattie became.

Gina stood in the shade of an alder tree greeting family members and friends. Many faces were unknown to her, as they were part of Mattie's vast circle of companions.

Bryan appeared alone. He wandered over to her and said, "Gina, words can't express the sorrow I feel for both of us, but especially for you. You raised Mattie all these years alone. My regret is that I didn't get to know our son better." He looked down to wipe away a tear.

"Thank you, Bryan. Your words mean a lot."

He left, and others waited patiently to speak to Gina.

"I'm so sorry for your loss. Mattie was an amazing guy," said Anthony, one of Mattie's coworkers at his part-time job.

"Thank you. I agree with you about the amazing part."

There seemed to be an endless line of consolatory words and hugs; all were the same, stating what a wonderful person Mattie was. While many times people say this as a perfunctory response at a person's loss, this was not the case. These words were truly heartfelt.

"How are you holding up so well?" asked Gina's brother, Ted, as he put his arms around her shoulders.

"I have a peace about where Mattie is. That makes all the difference in the world."

The service began with "First Love," a Chris Tomlin song sung by a close friend of Mattie's. Sidney's rendition of it brought tears to the eyes of many.

Pastor Mark began his remarks. "I can't think of a more fitting song than the one just sung to summarize Matthew Paul Hensley's life. Jesus Christ was Matthew's, or—as we better know him—Mattie's first love. I have known Mattie since the age of seven. I have watched him grow over the years from a boy into a man. During those years, his searching led him to the Lord. Mattie placed his faith in his Lord and Savior. He tried to live a life congruent with those teachings. He attempted to show compassion and kindness in his daily interactions with others."

Pastor Mark continued speaking for several more minutes. He concluded by saying, "Don't mourn the loss of our dear brother. Feel blessed that you had the privilege of sharing a relationship with him. Know with certainty that Mattie's job on

Earth was complete. He is now celebrating in a heavenly home that we cannot even begin to fathom the grandeur of."

Gina listened in amazement. Pastor Mark's words reiterated what Bart/Mattie had told her about how "his job was finished." Gina had not shared with a single soul her encounter that morning in Aroma Coffee. How could Pastor Mark know that?

After the last handshake and hug were exchanged, Gina said, "Abby, I'm exhausted."

"I understand—me too. How about grabbing a bite to eat, then heading back to our hotel?"

"Sounds like a great suggestion. Let's see if Emma would like to join us."

Emma was standing at the gravesite with little Travis. The sod had been replaced, and in a few weeks' time, a headstone would mark Mattie's earthly resting place. For the time being, the variegated blossoms of the floral arrangement were the sole marker of where the remains of her dear son lay.

Gina put her arms around the younger woman. No words were exchanged, just the simple embrace. They remained like that for several minutes.

"Emma, would you and Travis like to join us for a bite to eat? Abby and I are both ravenous and exhausted from today."

"Thank you. I'd like that."

"Travis, what do you think?"

"That would be great! Can we get ice cream afterwards?"

"Of course. We can even go to your favorite place."

After a dinner of hamburgers and French fries at The Bear, one of the spots Travis and Mattie enjoyed, the group ended up at Chico Confections for the promised after-dinner treat. As Travis consumed his chocolate-chocolate chip cone, the others discussed the remaining arrangements. Gina would stay behind in Chico for several more days to pack up Mattie's belongings. Abby needed to return to work, as she had already used a chunk of her vacation time.

"Emma, have you decided what you will do during the rest of summer?" Gina asked.

"Well, Travis will be with his dad next week. Jake is taking him to Disneyland for a few days. You can imagine how excited Travis is about that!"

Nodding her head in agreement, Gina said, "It will be good for him to have a diversion right now. Mattie's passing is a lot for one so young to handle."

"Yes, it is. I suppose I'll start looking for a teaching position, sending out resumes."

"This might be the perfect time for that. There are always those teachers who make a last-minute decision to retire; they're enjoying summer so much that the thought of returning to the classroom is too much to bear. I've known a few myself."

"Let's hope that's the case up here," said Emma.

⤜⤜⤛⤛

As Gina and Abby said their goodbyes the following morning, Abby looked her friend in the eye and stated, "Gina, you call me any time day or night if you want to talk, or if you need anything. I'm here for you."

"I know. You have done so much already. How can I ever thank you?"

"You would do the same for me. That's what best friends are for."

Gina nodded her head in agreement. She hugged her friend. "I love you. Drive safely, and don't forget to text me when you've made it home."

"I will, 'Mom,'" Abby said, laughing.

Chapter 11

The thought of going through Mattie's things and packing them up was almost overwhelming. Fortunately, Gina's brother Ted had driven Gina's car up to Chico for her, so Gina now had transportation. Ted had even been thoughtful enough to pick up some packing boxes and paper, knowing that she would need both.

Gina drove to the small apartment that Mattie rented on Nord Avenue. Where had time gone? It seemed just like yesterday that she had driven up to Chico with Mattie to help settle him into his first apartment. There had been several other moves over the years that Gina assisted in. He never had many belongings, but he did have quite a collection of books. Mattie was an avid reader and always accumulated a few more on various topics, especially history.

Each person seems to have his own unique scent he carries with him—one that evokes that person's face upon smelling it. Walking into the apartment, Gina was struck by the distinctive aroma of Mattie lingering in the air. It was as though he had never left; his presence remained.

She gazed around the room with its simple furnishings. A desk with a laptop stood against one wall, with several pictures of Emma and Travis atop it. A ceiling-high bookcase stood against the opposite wall. As typical of Mattie, the shelves were lined with books. A leather couch dominated much of the room. A book he had been reading was tossed on it, along with some paperwork. To think these were the last words Mattie had been pondering prior to his accident.

Gina glanced at the title of the book: *Unbroken*. She remembered hearing about the book, then the movie when it came out. It was the story of Louis Zamperini and what he endured during his captivity in a Japanese prison camp. With Mattie's love of history, it didn't surprise Gina that Mattie would be reading this. He admired those who showed great perseverance during difficult times. Hmm, but hadn't he? Turning it over, Gina read the book description on the back: a story of perseverance, resiliency, and forgiveness. Her son had demonstrated all of those throughout his life; perhaps that was why he was dearly loved by so many. Putting the book in her bag, Gina resolved to read it at some later time. She continued to harbor unforgiveness toward the drunk driver who killed her son. That needed to be dealt with.

Walking into the bedroom, Gina noticed again that simplicity was paramount; the only furnishings were a bed, dresser, andnightstand. She opened the closet door to find neatly hung shirts, pants, and a suit. A leather bomber jacket was tucked in the very back, a present from her brother Ted to Mattie. Mattie often received military memorabiliaor books on World War II, as that was the topic his master's degree focused on.

While Gina wanted to linger and gaze at every item Mattie possessed, she also knew that she needed to tackle the job at hand. Mattie's belongings had to be out of the apartment by the end of the month so it could be readied for the next tenant.

Gina began emptying the contents of the closet. Most of the clothing could be donated to a charity. She folded shirts and put them into the large plastic bags she had brought along. One shirt in particular caught her eye—a black CSU shirt, just like the one Bart wore that day they met in Aroma Coffee. *I need to keep this one,* Gina thought to herself. She pulled a hooded sweatshirt out of the closet and paused to inhale its aroma, the fragrance of Mattie. She would never tire of that smell. *Maybe Emma would like this.*

Once finished with the shirts, Gina began taking pants off their hangers. She decided to check pockets before stuffing them into bags, as she knew from past experience Mattie often left miscellaneous things in them. She found a couple of ticket stubs from recent movies he had attended, but nothing more.

Gina surveyed her work; she had already filled six large bags with clothing, so she decided to lug those to the car before continuing further. One by one, Gina carried the bags out and placed them in the back of her SUV. *This is going to take some time,* Gina thought to herself. *And I haven't even looked at the number of books Mattie has or what's in the kitchen.*

Tackling the dresser next wasn't bad until Gina came to Mattie's junk drawer—the one he kept mementos in from the many special events in his life. There were award ribbons from races he had run in; photos of different events at Chico State; ticket stubs from concerts he had attended, and his Eagle Scout award pins. Gina recalled that day clearly. Mattie had worked so hard to complete his Eagle Scout project. When he received his special pin, she received one as well. She kept that tucked away in a drawer at home. *Ha,* she thought. *I'm not much different from my son!*

The morning had passed quickly. Bags were lined up in the hallway, as Gina's car was nearly full from the previous loads she had stowed in it. *Time for a break and a bit of lunch,* she thought. She remembered that the small shopping center down the street had a pizza joint in it. *A slice to go sounds good.*

After a bit of nourishment, Gina began tackling the bookshelf. Mattie was a voracious reader, and volumes of books on myriad subject matter filled its shelves. Thankfully Mattie had grouped the books by topic, which made it easier for Gina to pack. *Emma can browse these later to see if there are any she would like to have.*

Gina had nearly finished pulling books from the top shelf when she discovered a small, leather-bound book. Curious as to what it was, Gina opened it, realizing immediately that she had come upon Mattie's personal journal. *Should I read it? Will that be invading his privacy?*

Gina decided to do so. She began reading:

The days after Kellie's phone call had been devastating, ones Mattie could hardly remember. He seemed to be living in a daze, just going through the motions. A buddy, Anthony, told Mattie about a Bible study group meeting on campus.

"Come on, Matt. Check it out. There's a lot of good stuff happening at Christian Challenge like fellowship, get-togethers, and encouragement. What do you have to lose? Pastor Phil is real; he's not one of these phonies you so often hear about."

"Alright, maybe this one time."

Mattie did go and found himself drawn to it. The students met weekly. Mattie felt something come alive in himself that he hadn't experienced in a long time. He couldn't wait to delve into the Word and go over his weekly study. Gradually the pain from Kellie began to subside. While a scar remained, it was fading with the passage of time.

As a Christian, Mattie knew that he was a minority on campus. Other students often ridiculed the small group that met across from Holt Hall. He didn't care; Christian Challenge was a salve to his broken heart and soul.

Gina stopped reading, remembering that time so well. She knew her son felt great loss and betrayal from Kellie. Gina skipped a few pages ahead:

The semester came to an end, but Mattie continued to live and work near the college. One June morning while walking downtown, he ran into Kellie.

"Hi Kellie," he said. "How are things going?"

Kellie looked down, her face reddening a bit. "Matt, I never meant to hurt you. Things with Rico just sort of happened."

"Yeah, well … Are you going home over the summer?"

"I'm working for my dad. He has a gig at one of the offices in Menlo Park lined up for me. It will be good to be home with friends and family."

"Good luck with the job. Maybe I'll see you next semester." He smiled and walked away.

Another chapter of his life had come to an end. This had been a painful one, but one he felt he had learned from. He realized that while he and Kellie had much in common and enjoyed each other's company, she was not the woman he would have wanted to spend the rest of his life with. If it hadn't been for her deception while abroad, Mattie would never have met Pastor Phil and the others at Christian Challenge. How different his life would have been. "As a follower of Jesus Christ, it must affect how I live my life daily," Gina read aloud. Tears welled up in her eyes as she read those words. Truly Mattie had taken them to heart. "Oh Lord, you use the bitter times of our lives to mold us and sweeten our spirit so it's more like your own." She witnessed that first hand in the life of her son.

More reading would have to wait until later as Gina tucked the journal into her bag. The remaining bookshelves needed emptying. Gina set to work and continued throughout much of the afternoon. With a sigh of exhaustion, she said, "This will have to do for today." She surveyed the disarray in the apartment, with boxes of books and bags of clothing sitting everywhere.

After a quick phone call to Emma, Gina decided to dine at the hotel restaurant and make an early evening of it. Emma promised to help Gina sort through more books and kitchen items the following day. "See if you can borrow a few strong guys to help with loading up all those boxes of books," quipped Gina.

Emma laughed at that. "Mattie did love his books."

Gina settled into bed and began perusing her son's journal once more. There was so much of his life as an adult that was an enigma to her. Before she knew it, she had nodded off with the journal on her chest.

In her dream, Mattie was once again a child and they were on their way to school. It was a cool April morning as Gina drove

Mattie to school before heading to her own classroom several miles away.

"Hey Mattie, a penny for your thoughts," Gina said, as the boy seemed so distant. "Anything you want to talk about?"

"It's Russell. He's been having a really hard time at school because he's kind of different."

Gina nodded knowingly. Mattie had mentioned Russell to her before. It sounded like Russell might be slightly autistic, and other kids played on that difference to torment him. "Russell is so lucky to have you as a friend, Mattie. You know that, right?"

"Yeah, I suppose I'm his only friend. Why do kids have to be like that? Russell is cool once you get to know him."

"Unfortunately, it's human nature. People frequently treat those different from themselves unkindly."

As they pulled up in front of the school, Gina gave Mattie a quick hug and a "Have a good day" before he was out the door.

Later that afternoon, as Gina signed Mattie out from his school daycare, she noticed that Mattie seemed more subdued than usual. "Hey buddy, how was your day?" she asked.

Mattie looked down before answering, "Not good."

"What happened?"

"Some of the other kids at recess grabbed Russell's hat. When he demanded it back, they teased him with 'Come and get it.' Then they ran the other direction and tossed it to someone else when Russell was nearby. Mom, I was so mad at them. I ran into one of them, Carter, and knocked him to the ground. Mrs. Wilson sent me to the principal's office."

"Mattie, I understand that you were angry about Russell being taunted, but hurting others is not the solution."

"I know."

"How about if you and I add this to our prayer list? I can think of someone else who was made fun of many years ago."

"You mean Jesus, right?"

"I do."

"You're probably right." For the first time that day, Mattie felt like smiling. He had hoped that someone else was looking out for Russell beside himself.

Gina woke up with a start, the light still blazing in her room and the journal lying on the floor. Her thoughts were a bit fuzzy. She had been in the car with Mattie heading to school. She remembered there had been a problem with one of the other kids in his class. Oh, that seemed so long ago. She searched her memory, trying to determine whether this incident had really happened or whether reading the journal had induced it. Unsure, Gina fell into a deep slumber once more.

The following morning, Gina met Emma at Mattie's apartment. Gina appreciated having an extra pair of hands to help with the task at hand, as there was still much to do.

Emma eyed the boxes and bags lined up in the hallway. "You have been busy."

"My back will attest to that," agreed Gina.

The women set to work emptying the remaining shelves and packing up the books. Emma selected several books that she would like to read.

"Any suggestions what we should do with these?" Gina asked.

Emma looked up from working. "Perhaps we could donate them to the library. They have an annual sale of used books; they use the proceeds to expand their literacy program."

"That sounds like a wonderful idea. Do they happen to pick up books?" Gina asked as she mentally calculated the weight of each box.

"I'll check."

Once finished, they headed into the kitchen. They began emptying the cupboards of the mismatched cups, glasses, and plates. "A true college student," remarked Gina, noticing how no two items seemed to match.

"I'd like to keep these, if you don't mind," said Emma, pointing to a couple of mugs. "They would be something for Travis and me to remember Mattie by."

"Absolutely. Take anything you'd like."

The remaining cupboards were emptied of miscellaneous items. Emma paused to view the pizza pans and bowls. "We had some great times here with Mattie making dinner for us, usually pizza and always ice cream for dessert." Tears welled up in her eyes as she spoke.

Gina wrapped her arms around her. "It's okay, Emma. We both miss him and always will. One day at a time, right?"

Emma nodded her head in agreement, tears spilling down her face.

"How about we drop these bags off somewhere then grab a bite of lunch? We can decide on what to do with Mattie's furniture later."

"That sounds good."

After depositing the items at a local charity, the pair wandered into a sandwich shop. The heat of the day was setting in, and it was bound to be another scorcher. Gina appreciated the reprieve she felt immediately upon walking through the door. Looking around, she noticed that the ceiling was covered with tin tiles, leftovers from another era, while one wall was pieced together out of worn bricks.

"What a quaint place this is with the old tiles and bricks."

Emma nodded her head in agreement. "Most of these buildings date from the late 1800s or early 1900s. That's part of their charm."

While stirring cream into her iced coffee, Gina asked, "Have you thought about how you're going to fill your days besides job hunting? We've been pretty busy the past couple of weeks, but when all this is over, the finality of Mattie's death will really hit home."

Emma nodded in agreement. "I know. Perhaps I could become involved in an organization—something similar to what Mattie was doing, though I'm not sure what."

"What about if you volunteered at a woman's shelter? You would probably be great working with women; you seem to have a lot of empathy for them."

"Yes, possibly."

When their turkey and avocado sandwiches arrived, the women delved into them and their chatting stopped. Gina noticed that the shop had filled up with many college-age girls. She wondered whether their lives were as carefree as their appearances indicated. Gina had reexamined her own thinking with all that had happened recently and mused: *How often do we wear masks that belie our true hurts or needs?*

She thought of Emma, as well as Natalie with her abusive boyfriend. At that moment, Gina promised herself she would take the time needed to invest in others, to be the salve that Mattie had been in the lives of so many.

Chapter 12

The apartment had finally been emptied of its contents, with most of the furniture donated to a battered woman's shelter. Gina knew that Mattie would have liked that. She and Emma stood in the empty apartment one last time before returning the key to the apartment manager. It seemed that all traces of the once vibrant spirit who had inhabited the apartment had been wiped clean. Both women stood in silence. Mattie was gone, never coming back.

'This is so hard, letting go of all the memories we once had here," Emma murmured.

"I know, honey. I feel the same way."

Both observed a silent goodbye. Now would come the painful process of moving on. *Which is harder, saying goodbye or moving on?* thought Gina.

A common bond had formed between Gina and Emma, that being the one shared by true heartache. Gina treasured the relationship that had grown out of their mutual loss. She considered Emma and Travis part of her immediate family. "Wait till Christmas, when you get to spend time with my brother, Ted. You will experience firsthand his love for goading one into a debate."

Emma laughed. "I can hardly wait. Mattie described Christmas with his Uncle Ted in vivid detail to me."

✦✦✦ ✦✦✦

Gina returned to the Bay Area. She understood that both she and Emma had to deal with their grief individually and heal at their own pace. Healing could not be rushed, and the process would be different for each of them. Gina joined a grief support group where she could share the pain of her loss with others who had experienced loss of some kind. She became a member of a club she had no intention of ever joining: being a parent whose child has preceded them in death.

After returning from an evening session, Gina thought she would check on Emma. "Hi Emma—it's Gina. How are you doing?"

"I'm doing okay."

"How are you *really* doing? I know about 'okay.' I'm the queen of okay."

"I'm struggling. There's too much time left in each day, and that's when my thoughts return to Mattie and what might have been."

"Honey, I understand. Remember our conversation that day in Starbucks about joining a grief support group? Maybe you should consider doing so. I found one that's been helping me cope with my loss." Gina recounted her own experience with the group.

"I may do that. It sounds like what I need."

Changing the subject, Gina asked, "Any leads on a teaching job?"

"Well, I have two interviews scheduled for next week."

"That's wonderful! What grades?"

"Second and fourth grade. I would be fine with either. At this point, I need to focus on something else rather than the emptiness I feel inside."

"Emma, do you remember our discussion about continuing on where Mattie left off?"

"Yeah."

"Maybe that's where your focus should be—on others. It seems that when we give, we in turn receive—a law of reciprocity of sorts. Our focus is off ourselves. Figure out what gives you joy, gets you out of bed each morning. That's your gift, someone once told me. Pour that passion into the lives around you to bring healing and make the world a better place."

"I don't know whether there is anything left inside of me to give. Aside from Travis, I feel so empty inside."

"You know the deep faith that Mattie had? Now is the time for you to embrace that, cry out to the Lord above. He hears you and is aware of every tear you have shed. I promise you that."

The following morning, Gina was lost in thought as she planted gaily colored zinnias in clay pots around her backyard. Her garden had been ignored much of the summer, and she knew that expending this effort would bring her joy with the profusion of color. *This* brought her joy. What were her words to

Emma, which had also been the words Bart had spoken to her? Find what brings you joy, gets you going each day.

Gina delighted in the sights and fragrances of her garden, whether it was the aromatic lavender or the seemingly cheerful sunflowers. She could bring bouquets of flowers to nursing homes; that would undoubtedly brighten someone's day. But there had to be something more. Gina racked her brain as she dug holes for the purple and pink phlox she would place around her walkway. Besides her garden, her son had brought her endless joy. She had peace and an assurance that she would see him again, as she had accepted Jesus as Lord of her life.

Her *son*. That was it.

She knew what her calling was.

Chapter 13

Gina had heard about crisis pregnancy centers, but knew very little about what they actually did. Now was the time to learn more. She opened her laptop to see what organizations were in the Bay Area and whether they needed volunteers.

Locating a Pregnancy Counseling Center in a nearby town, Gina clicked on the link to read about it and the services it furnished. Aside from offering options to someone who unexpectedly becomes pregnant, the center provided counseling, a certain amount of prenatal care, and clothing and diapers for the newborn. How she would have benefited from something like that 26 years ago, as she thought back to her own unplanned pregnancy.

Scanning the website further, Gina found the section detailing the center's needs, especially volunteers. "That's it." She wasted no time in shooting off an email expressing her interest and contact information.

Two days later, Gina's cell phone buzzed. A woman identifying herself as Barbara Simpson was on the phone. Her call was in response to Gina's query. She scheduled an appointment for Gina to come by later that afternoon to view the pregnancy center and complete an application.

Nervous excitement filled Gina as she maneuvered her car through city traffic. She finally located the discreet building surrounded by blooming crepe myrtle trees. Walking through the front door, Gina noticed how serene the front office appeared. Perhaps she was expecting something more akin to the drama surrounding abortion clinics, or at least what she had heard on the news.

A petite brunette arose and introduced herself as Barbara Simpson. "It's so nice to meet you, Gina," she said while shaking hands. "Let's go to my office where we can talk privately."

Following Barbara into a small but tastefully decorated office, Barbara inquired as to how Gina had become interested in volunteering at the pregnancy center.

Gina briefly related the situation she faced 26 years ago and the choice she almost made. She continued that her son had recently passed away, and what a blessing he had been to her and countless others over the years.

"I hope to encourage other moms to choose life," Gina finished. "We never know the impact that one life will have on another's."

Barbara listened intently the entire time, never once averting Gina's gaze. "That is quite a story you have to tell. Have you ever thought of putting it into words? I'm sure it would encourage many."

"I haven't and I'm not sure if I could do so at this point; the wound is still fresh with Mattie's passing."

"I understand. Maybe some time in the future. Anyway, let me show you around and describe our volunteer opportunities."

Barbara passed several closed doors. "These are where the ladies—or clients, if you will—meet with our counselors. Frequently the clients feel similar to the way you felt so many years ago. They need a listening ear and the assurance that there are other choices asidefrom abortion."

Another door led to an examination room. "We have doctors and nurses who volunteer their time to perform exams, ultrasounds, and other services."

Continuing down the hall, Gina spotted a cheerful room filled with a vast assortment of layette items, rivaling anything seen in Macy's. Newborn outfits of varying colors hung on a rack, while blankets in hues of blues and pinks were placed on shelves.

Barbara noted Gina's wonder. "This is my favorite room. Each outfit indicates that there is a new life going home to a loving family. Every mom receives a basket of diapers and wipes, formula, bottles, and several outfits for her little one as a way of getting her started in motherhood. Our volunteers here have so much fun shopping for the items, and we have several women who devote their time to crocheting blankets for the babies. Of course, most of our clothing comes in as donations from the public."

"How wonderful!" Gina enthused. "I'm sure it's very much appreciated."

"We try to help our new moms in whatever way we can."

Gina returned to Barbara's office to complete the necessary paperwork. "You will need to go through an orientation. We offer one on either the first or third Saturday of each month from 10–12. Our first orientation begins next week. Would you like me to add your name to our list of attendees?"

"Please do. I'm a teacher and school will be resuming for me soon, but Saturdays will work out just fine."

Gina left the Pregnancy Counseling Center with mixed emotions. She wanted to encourage others to choose life, but could she do so with her own loss still an open wound?

Chapter 14

*G*ina picked up her cell phone, noticing that Emma was calling. "Hi Emma, how are you doing today?"

"I feel so much better as I now know what my gift is and what I'm supposed to do with it. My other great news is that I have a teaching job; I was offered the fourth grade position!"

"That is absolutely wonderful news. I'm so happy for you."

Emma told Gina all about the school where she would be teaching. Then she launched into how her own relationship with Jake started her thinking; there were probably many women in Chico or the area in similar situations. She called one domestic violence service that worked with victims and their children. Emma spoke with Leah, who stated that a training class would be starting later that month for new volunteers.

"Gina, I'm so excited. The organization asks that you volunteer at least three hours a week and continue doing so for six months. They want to develop some continuity between the volunteers and those living on the premises. That's something I can manage while teaching and still being a mom to Travis."

"Emma, that sounds perfect for you. Any idea as to what you'd be doing?"

"I'm thinking about working with the children. They need people to assist with playtime and creating various activities for the kids, especially while moms are attending house meetings or group counseling sessions."

The women chatted for a few more minutes before hanging up. Gina smiled and whispered a prayer of thanks. Two needs had been filled: the emptiness in Emma's spirit along with the childcare need at the domestic violence center.

❧❧❧

Gina began her trainings at the Pregnancy Counseling Center. She was amazed to hear of the number of women visiting the site to learn of options other than abortion. While the ultimate goal was to encourage each woman to choose life rather than end it, there was no condemnation if they did otherwise. One of the offerings at the center dealt with post-abortion counseling.

Some of the volunteer opportunities included staffing phones, greeting clients, and sorting through the maternity clothing that had been donated to the center. Gina felt that answering phones would be the perfect fit for her.

School had resumed. The transition between summer and the start of the new school year had gone smoothly. None of the usual remorse over the things Gina had left unfinished or not had an opportunity to do existed. Instead, Gina chose to focus on the fullness of each day.

The days were busy. Second graders truly are first graders in September, just a bit taller. Gina resolved to retain a peace about her, regardless of what was happening with her students, their parents, or co-workers.

Sitting in the staff room one day at lunch, another teacher named Maggie began her usual litany of complaints: her students didn't remember a thing from the previous grade; Brad, her husband, had played golf all weekend while she was stuck doing errands with her own children, and on it continued. Gina began drowning it out then remembered the promise she had made to listen.

"I can only imagine how frustrated you felt, especially after dealing with kids at school all week. Have you mentioned to your husband that a break would be welcome?"

"Uh, well not exactly." Maggie was speechless that someone had listened as well as validated her feelings.

"I remember those days. While I adored Mattie and spending time with him, there were occasions when I needed an hour or two just to decompress. Being a parent is a tough job."

Others in the room nodded in agreement, amazed at Gina's candor knowing full well the loss of her only son.

"Let me know if I can help you in any way," Gina said, smiling at Maggie.

"Thank you. I appreciate it."

Gina beamed inwardly as she strode back to her classroom.

Tuesday nights were reserved for Gina to volunteer at the Pregnancy Counseling Center, as she typically didn't have after- school meetings. This one particular night, Gina entered the center feeling especially weary. What a day she had had at school with behavior problems at recess and a class that insisted on chatting rather than listening during her math lesson.

"Hi Melanie," Gina called out to another volunteer as she entered the center.

"Hi Gina," was the response back.

Immediately Gina felt a calm replace the anxiety of the day. Most of the other volunteers had left for the evening. A handful staffed phones or remained to pray for their clients.

"How have things been going today?"

"It's been fairly quiet," replied Melanie. "Oh, I spoke too soon," she said while picking up the ringing phone.

Gina laughed. Before she knew it, her phone was buzzing as well.

"Pregnancy Counseling Center. Gina speaking," she said.

A voice on the other line asked, "Is this where you go to get an abortion?"

"No, we share with you what other alternatives are available beside abortion."

"Okay, thanks," said the voice; she sounded ready to hang up.

"Please don't hang up. Let's talk. Can you tell me your situation?"

Before realizing it, the caller, a sixteen-year-old girl named Lydia, explained that she was pregnant by her boyfriend, and that her parents would be furious if they found out.

"Oh, honey, I know exactly how you feel." Gina proceeded to tell Lydia about her own experience about being pregnant and a boyfriend who demanded that she terminate the pregnancy. Instead, she kept the baby, and what a joy he had been to her.

"Your son, does he know all this?" Lydia asked.

"He did. Mattie passed away a few months ago." Gina felt a lump in her throat as she said that.

"Wow. I'm sorry for your loss. It must be hard."

"It has been. But if I had that abortion, I never would have had those 25 years with him."

Gina ended the conversation with Lydia by persuading her to come in the following day to speak with one of their counselors to explore other options.

When it was time to close the center for the evening, Gina shared with Melanie a bit of her conversation with Lydia.

"Gina, that's amazing. I think you should be one of our counselors," enthused Melanie.

"Ha—I just started and you're trying to promote me already," Gina laughed as they walked out the door together.

Driving home that evening, Gina uttered a prayer of thanks for the Lord steering Lydia her way. "Please Lord, give Lydia the courage to choose life, and help me put aside my own sadness momentarily and be available to those who need a word of encouragement."

Chapter 15

The days seemed to be a flurry of activity between Gina's second graders at school, volunteering at the pregnancy center, and attempting to be more present for those in her immediate sphere of influence. Memories of Mattie continued to invade her thoughts. Gina dealt with those painful memories by talking to others at the grief support group she attended and by writing letters to God in her journal.

She learned that one must go through a process of healing from grief, and there are various stages. One might go through all the stages, or just a few. Gina had experienced many herself, ranging from disbelief to anger to unfairness and anxiety. Now she struggled with loneliness.

While Gina and Emma had developed a close bond in their relationship and Gina thought of Travis as her own grandson, Gina longed for the phone calls she used to receive from Mattie. His exuberance would brighten the dreariest of days. How she missed his, "Hi Mom, how's it going?" He would elaborate on the latest happenings at work, in Chico, or in his relationships.

Abby called regularly, as did others, but it wasn't the same. There was a void that needed filling, especially in the early evenings around the time Mattie had often called.

The grief support group Gina attended met weekly at a nearby community church. Claire, the facilitator, had been leading such groups for several years. While not having lost anyone close to her, Claire had experienced much grief vicariously through the lives of those she interacted with. Tonight's topic dealt with forgiveness: forgiving others and one's self.

"As one travels down the path of grief, it is not uncommon to blame others or oneself for your loved one's death."

Other women in the group nodded their heads in agreement.

"I want to dispel that misconception right now. The Lord has told us in Psalms 139:16 that '…the days allotted to me had all been recorded in your book before any of them ever began.' He was not surprised by the circumstances surrounding the loss of your loved one. He had ordained it for whatever reason He chose."

Some of the women sitting in Gina's group looked up in surprise. Why would a loving God allow or even plan for a child to precede a parent in death?

Claire continued, "While you won't have answers for the many questions you have on Earth, one day you will. In the meantime, I can assure you that God uses everything He allows into our lives for His glory and good. There is a purpose for our suffering, and He alone can bring beauty out of these circumstances if you allow Him to do so."

Gina nodded her head in agreement. Hadn't Bart suggested as much to her that day in Chico when they spoke?

Another woman at the table stood up in anger. "That's too hard for me to accept that a supposedly loving God would allow this kind of pain into my life, the loss of my young daughter." She grabbed her purse, storming out of the room.

"It's okay that Sandra feels that way. Remember, anger and disbelief are part of grief," Claire assured them. "That's why we are walking this path together, to support one another."

Claire commented on the part that faith takes. "Think about those in the Bible who experienced loss. Do any come to mind?"

Several names were mentioned, from Naomi to King David and Job.

"Job, yes. He suffered great loss: his children, his wealth, his servants, not to mention the physical affliction which was heaped upon him. Yet he survived and even prospered later on. Why was that?"

"Because of his faith?" one woman volunteered.

"Exactly. He knew the kind of God he worshipped and served. He had learned in years past that God is faithful. Hold on to your faith as you travel this journey. It's imperative to the path you are now on."

The group broke into discussions at each individual table. Those who felt comfortable doing so shared how she was feeling, or what she was struggling with at the moment.

It took all the courage one woman could muster to get out of bed each day, shower, and dress. "I want to hide under the covers, hoping it will all go away—that it's just some sort of bad dream. I understand that I must take baby steps in healing. Maybe I will reach the point where I want to cook a meal once more instead of eating frozen dinners."

Some nodded in agreement. Another woman, Tina, related the physical exhaustion she felt being a single parent after losing her husband to cancer. "I now have all the responsibilities we once shared together heaped on me, besides shouldering my grief and my children's. There are days I feel that I just can't go on."

Claire gathered the group back together to give them an assignment for the following session. "In Isaiah 45:3, the Lord says, 'He will give you treasures of darkness.' Before next week's meeting, I want you to ponder those words in light of what we discussed earlier, about what good can come out of your current situation and the part faith plays in it. Many of you may only see darkness at the moment or for the days to come. But try anyway. Embrace suffering—don't fight it—and you may find yourself surprised."

Treasures of darkness. Hmmm, that is something to contemplate, thought Gina. She wondered how Emma was faring on her own journey and vowed to call her the following day.

Chapter 16

It was nearly Christmas—the first Christmas without her beloved son. Gina felt a pang of fear clutch at her heart, and her breathing became more rapid. "No, I'm not going there. I'm not giving in to those feelings of fear and loss," she told herself. How could she create new memories, establish new traditions without Mattie?

Gina thought back to the previous Christmas. It had been more subdued since her sister had passed away two years earlier, leaving Ted without a sparring partner. While Ted attempted to engage Mattie in some topic of debate, Mattie never fell for Ted's ploys. Ted would look a bit forlorn, but invariably find a new topic of discussion even if it was something as bland as the rising price of gas in California.

Mattie and Emma had been seeing each other for several months, but Emma felt it was important that she spend Christmas with her family, as her father had recently been diagnosed with cancer. Travis would be spending the holiday with his father and new stepmother.

While Mattie made the trip down from Chico and they enjoyed their time together, Gina knew his thoughts were on Emma and her family. She understood. Nevertheless, she maintained their usual tradition of attending a Christmas Eve service followed by French onion soup, crusty bread, a tossed salad, and a wide assortment of cookies. Mattie loved the spritz and pinwheel cookies that Gina baked each holiday season. He was the sole reason she baked at all; heavens knew she didn't need it, with her expanding waistline.

Christmas Day held its own special traditions, with a steam train and tiny village being set up beneath the tree. Of course the train tooted and emitted steam as it chugged around the turns winding through the Victorian village.

Peeking in stockings always preceded breakfast. Presents would wait until later in the day, when Ted, Gina's bachelor brother, joined them. Mattie always feigned amazement at the items he pulled out of his stocking. "Mom, how did you know I needed an Eddie Bauer flashlight?" he would ask.

She remembered laughing and saying, "Well, you do have power outages in Chico, don't you? It's better to be prepared."

He would give her a hug and empty the remaining contents out of his stocking. How she loved watching him do so regardless of how old he was. Then it was on to breakfast, a feast in itself.

Special Christmas plates were set out on the red-covered table; snowflakes and green pine trees adorned the rims. Gina heaped generous portions of scrambled eggs mixed with cheese, sausage, and garlic potatoes onto Mattie's plate. Homemade cranberry muffins awaited everyone on the table, along with mixed fruit.

"Mom," he protested, "I'm not 200 pounds—or at least, not yet."

"I can only imagine how you eat in Chico."

"I eat just fine. See, I'm still here," he would insist.

Dinner, presents, and Ted would follow. While there were times Gina dreaded the afternoons with her brother, as his behavior was so unpredictable—and at time just embarrassing—he was, after all, her only brother. He had been a faithful and loving uncle to Mattie over the years. He was more of a father to his nephew than Mattie's own father had been. Gina doubted that Ted realized the gratitude she felt toward him for that gift.

What to do about this Christmas? She picked up the phone to call Abby. "Hi there, stranger. What are you doing this year for Christmas?"

"Peter is coming over for Christmas dinner. He's spending Christmas Eve with Nina's family. Things appear to be getting serious between those two."

"Ted will be here for Christmas dinner. I'm hoping Emma and Travis will be as well, though I haven't asked them yet. I have nothing planned for Christmas Eve, do you?"

"No, not at the moment."

"What would you think about having an open house of sorts for those who don't have a place to go?"

"I think that would be a wonderful idea, and I would help you in any way."

"Great. Now who do we invite?"

The two planned food, a guest list, and discussed how to open the night up to friends and co-workers. "I think this will really work," Gina said excitedly as she hung up.

Her next phone call was to Emma. Emma said that she and Travis would love to join them Christmas Day. As Jake had visitation with Travis last year, it was her turn to enjoy the holidays with him. She would spend Christmas Eve and morning with her family, then drive down after breakfast to visit with Gina and Ted for the rest of the day.

Gina felt excitement building within her. "Alright Mattie, first thing's first. We need to find the perfect tree."

The following Saturday, Gina drove to a Christmas tree lot and examined the trees critically as she had often done with Mattie. "That one has a bare spot there. This one is too scrawny." Deciding upon the perfect tree—one that was just the right height, lacking in bare spots, and had ample branches to hang ornaments upon—Gina wonderedhow she was going to get it into the house, let alone set it up. "Maybe I can get Dave from next door to help me," she mused.

As Gina pulled up into her driveway, she viewed Dave walking toward his mailbox. "Dave—Dave!" She waved at him. "Can I borrow you for a few minutes?"

He ambled over and readily agreed to Gina's request for help. Lifting the tree off the roof of Gina's SUV, he remarked, "It looks like you have some tree here."

"It does seem perfect, doesn't it?"

In no time, Dave and Gina had the tree set up in the living room. "Dave, thank you so much for your help; I couldn't have done it without you."

"Any time," said Dave, grinning. "I suppose Cindy will want me to do the same thing at our house later today."

"The power of suggestion, I suppose," Gina laughed. Gina then told Dave about the Christmas Eve Open House, in case he knew of any singles or others spending Christmas alone.

"I do, in fact. That's a great idea."

"Please tell them they are welcome; the more the merrier. It's an impromptu celebration. Just come and enjoy."

Gina climbed into the attic of her home to retrieve boxes of Christmas lights and decorations. *Why does it seem a little more exhausting each year to lug all these boxes down? Maybe because I'm getting older?* she thought as she pushed wisps of gray hair off her forehead.

She untangled the strands of lights and hung them on the tree, carefully weaving the tiny bulbs in and out of the branches. Next came the ornaments. Gingerly lifting out the glass globes from Germany that her parents had given her so many years ago, Gina recalled tales of their first Christmas together. Those globes were all they could afford to hang on their own tree.

The next box brought tears to her eyes, as it contained ornaments that Mattie had made for her over the years—handprints stamped in clay from preschool, glass swirled balls from second grade, and so on. As she lifted each ornament out of its box, savoring the memory associated with it, she lovingly set it upon a bough of the tree. Her sweet boy was with her once more.

Not being able to contain herself any longer, Gina sat beside the tree and wept. How she missed him. The thought of never sharing another Christmas with her son nearly set off a panic attack. The pain inside her had subsided from that all-encompassing, not-able-to- breathe, feeling-dizzy sensation, but nevertheless, it lingered. She knew it would do so for some time. What would Claire at her grief support group say to do? *Remind yourself that God is faithful.* Bart would tell her to use her gifts. She was trying to do both, but she still struggled with her loss.

Gina eyed the balsam tree with its twinkling white lights. It was indeed a thing of beauty, and its fragrance permeated the house. How she loved that smell. The train encircling its base completed the look. She would start inviting others to her home for Christmas Eve as soon as she had hung the stockings on the mantel. That would have to come first.

Fingering the stocking that her own grandmother had lovingly stitched for Mattie to celebrate his first Christmas brought back a flood of memories. Her grandmother had stitched it out of red felt and embellished it with a snowman, angel, and tree, also out of felt. Gina knew that it was an act of love for her grandmother to make it, as her eyesight had deteriorated significantly. That made it all the more precious to her.

Gina placed Mattie's stocking in the spot where it hung each year; she vowed to continue doing so for Christmases to come. *Hmm, what can I put in there this year? Even though he's not physically here, I can just imagine his response when he looks inside.*

Surprisingly, the days leading up to Christmas were ones filled with joy. Gina decorated a small tree and brought it in to the Pregnancy Counseling Center. She did the same for the staff room at school. Gina noted that Maggie's attitude had improved; she complained much less about her husband or her students. Even more so, Gina stood staring, wide mouthed, when Maggie suggested that the staff collect presents for those children at school who would not be receiving any.

"Maggie, that's a wonderful idea. Maybe we can even have a small party of sorts—face painting, crafts, a few games."

"I'll ask Brad if he'll dress up as Santa."

Gina nearly choked when Maggie suggested that.

The staff rallied behind Maggie, and plans were made how to bless those who would not be having much of a Christmas. The day of the event turned out even better than they had hoped. Besides presents for the kids, a local tree lot had donated several trees. The children set to work designing their own ornaments, followed by cookie decorating, and finally a visit from Santa himself. The squeals of delight that followed were music to Gina's ears.

Brad played the part of Santa to a tee, and all the children were convinced they had just spoken with the man himself.

"Brad, thank you for bringing so much joy to our students. It will linger in their memories for some time, I am sure," said Gina.

"I think I enjoyed it as much as they did. If you do it again next year, let me know. I'd be glad to help out again."

Gina smiled and said, "I most certainly will. Thanks."

⟫⟫⟫ ⟪⟪⟪

It was Tuesday evening, the last one before Gina's Christmas break at school began. As usual she volunteered at the Pregnancy Counseling Center on Tuesdays. Tonight she manned both the front desk and the phones, as many of the volunteers were busy with holiday preparations. The door opened, and to Gina's surprise, in walked Lydia, the sixteen-year-old who had called about a possible abortion. Gina had not seen or heard anything from Lydia for a few months.

"Hi," said Lydia with a large tummy protruding from her coat. "I called Barbara earlier today. She said it would be okay if I came by to pick up a few more maternity clothes. I can hardly fit into the ones I have."

"Absolutely." Gina led Lydia to the back room, where maternity clothes were available to those needing them. "Lydia, you look wonderful! You decided to keep the baby?"

"Yeah. Miss Warren, the counselor I talked to, persuaded me to tell my parents. She said she would even be there with me for moral support if I wanted her to. My parents were pretty upset at first, but they said it's their grandchild, and they would help me care for it while I finish school."

"Lydia, I am so happy for you," Gina beamed.

"It's a girl. I decided to name her Rose, after my grandmother," Lydia said, smiling.

Gina gave the girl a hug and said to let her know if she needed help selecting clothes. Inwardly she was saying, "Yes, Lord!"

Chapter 17

*C*hristmas Eve arrived. The house glowed with candles, the lights upon the tree, and an unspoken presence. Abby helped Gina lay out a bountiful spread on the dining room table, including French onion soup, bread, a tossed salad, baked ham, potatoes, an assortment of cheeses and crackers, and or course, Gina's spritz and pinwheel cookies.

Gina surveyed the scene with the train chugging around the village and Mattie's stocking on the mantel. "Abby, this is nearly perfect."

"Nearly?" Abby questioned.

"We need guests."

Abby laughed. "They'll be arriving soon enough."

And they did. Gina answered the door to faces she had never seen before. She welcomed them into her home as if they were dear friends, and many became just that. Some were her age, some younger, many older. They all shared a common bond: needing to feel loved and a part of something on this special night.

After the last soul had departed, Abby sighed. "That was some party."

Smiling at her, Gina agreed. "Let's get this cleaned up. I have preparations to take care of for tomorrow before Emma, Travis, and Ted arrive."

In no time, dishes were washed and put away, leftovers stowed in the refrigerator or given to guests as they departed. After Abby said her goodbye, Gina sat by the lit tree taking in the serenity.

In the stillness of that moment, Gina experienced what it must have been like for Mary 2,000 years ago. All activity for the day had ceased, while a calm enveloped her. "I wonder if this is how you felt as you held your new babe close to you, savoring the peace and stillness all around you, if only for a moment." Gina too, savored that time, even though Mattie wasn't with her.

Deciding to read a devotional before heading off to bed, Gina opened *Our Daily Bread* to December 24. "Hope of the World" was the title. *How we all need hope,* she thought. *Not the world's kind of hope, but something greater.* As she often did, Gina underlined thoughts she wanted to remember or ponder. Her pencil slid between the cushions on the couch; thrusting her hand beneath them, she hoped to retrieve it, but instead came up empty-handed. Getting up from her cozy spot, Gina yanked the cushion off the couch. Staring up at her was a picture of Mattie, one from his elementary school days with the words written on it: *Merry Christmas, Mom. I love you, Mattie.* A big heart encircled his name.

"Oh," Gina uttered, covering her mouth with her hand as tears streamed down her cheeks. One last gift from her dearly loved son.

Christmas afternoon brought a flurry of excitement. Travis didn't want to budge from his spot near the tree; the sight of the train making its way through the village had him mesmerized. With each toot, he let out a gleeful sound.

Ted took it upon himself to entertain Travis. He explained how a steam engine worked, then suggested they try to build a train out of Legos. Ted knew that Mattie had a penchant for Legos, and a box of them was tucked away in a cupboard.

"Wow, do you think we can really make one?"

"Let's try," encouraged Ted.

While they worked on their project, Gina and Emma put the finishing touches on dinner: a juicy prime rib awaited carving, and rolls were popped into the oven for warming. Gina heaped garlic mashed potatoes into a serving dish, while Emma placed an assortment of other delights on the dining room table.

"Come on, guys. Dinner is ready."

As they held hands around the table, Gina asked Ted if he would say a blessing over the meal.

"Lord, we thank you for this food we are about to enjoy and for each person who is with us here today. We ask you to bless each of us in the year ahead. Amen."

Gina noticed that Ted did not mention any of the hardships or struggles they had endured during the past six months. She added a silent thanks for the Lord's strength and presence through all of it.

They enjoyed the sumptuous food and chatted. Ted, not missing an opportunity for debate, attempted to engage Travis in a discussion over superheroes. Gina ignored him and focused on Emma. "Tell me about your class and how the year is going."

"As you know, it's a lot. I mean, there's all the curriculum to learn, the lesson planning, papers to grade ... I never feel caught up."

"Welcome to teaching," Gina laughed. "The first year is the hardest, but it will become a bit easier, I promise. Here are a few shortcuts that have worked for me." Gina launched into an explanation as Emma took note.

"Before we open presents, it's a tradition in this house to make a toast to the New Year and mention some of the blessings from the year past. We are toasting with sparkling cider because Travis is not of legal drinking age," Gina said, smiling at Travis.

"Oh, man," he groaned.

"I'll start. I am thankful for my wonderful family," Gina said, looking at each person individually. "I'm especially thankful for my Lord and Savior, and His care during this past year."

Ted began, "I'm thankful for all of you, and that I have another man in the house." With that, he gave Travis a high-five.

"Thanks, Ted. Emma?"

Looking a bit shy, Emma responded, "I'm thankful for all of you, and the love and support you have shown Travis and me this past year."

"Here, here," chimed in Ted. "To the year ahead. Let's make it the best one yet, creating special memories along the way."

They clinked their glasses together, laughing and enjoying each other's presence. Cookies were passed, followed by slices of a Yule log that Emma had baked. Travis glowed, taking in the laughter and love emanating from the faces all around him.

"This is so good for him," Emma said, glancing toward Travis.

"It's good for all of us," agreed Gina.

Before long, Ted was urging them into the living room to open presents. "Come on, let's get going. I want to see what Santa brought me this year."

"With your behavior, you'll be lucky if he brought you anything," laughed Gina.

"Oohs and aahs" emanated as gifts were opened. One small package remained. It had Emma's name on it.

Emma looked at it curiously, as there was no indication as to who the giver was. She removed the ribbon and the tape holding the paper together to reveal a velvet box. Lifting the lid, she beheld Mattie's college ring. Looking up at Gina, she said, "Thank you, Gina. This means a lot to me. Mattie wore this constantly."

"You are most welcome, Emma. However, the gift is not from me."

Their eyes met, and a knowing look was exchanged between them. Come to think of it, Gina didn't remember that ring being with any of Mattie's things at the funeral home or in his apartment. Christmas is truly a time for miracles of all sizes and sorts.

Long after Ted had left and Travis was fast asleep in bed, Gina and Emma sat in the living room talking, enjoying the twinkle of the lights and the silence of the steam engine.

"I'm so glad that you and Travis were here; your presence truly made this a wonderful Christmas."

"I couldn't agree more. Your brother, Ted, is something."

"Yes, he is," laughed Gina. "*Something* describes Ted perfectly. With the New Year ahead of you, how are you doing?"

"I continue to take each day as it comes. You're right that being a part of a grief support group has helped so much. I have others to lean on. Teaching keeps me busy, as well as Travis."

"Both of those are full-time jobs," stated Gina. "But...I sense something more."

"I miss him. What can I say? I enjoy volunteering at the shelter. The kids are so needy; they absorb any kindness shown to them just like a sponge. In spite of all of that, there is an emptiness."

"Yes, I feel the same way," agreed Gina. "I think we will always miss Mattie, but eventually the sorrow and feelings of emptiness will fade."

"I hope you're right about the sorrow and emptiness fading."

Gina looked Emma squarely in the eyes. "In spite of all that's happened this year, we are blessed. I remind myself of that daily. My personal goal is to live my life so that I am a blessing to those around me. I have a role model to follow with Mattie."

"That's a great attitude to have. I should try to do the same."

The women continued talking until the wee hours. Yawning, Gina said, "I should let you get some sleep. Travis will probably be up early, and want to try out the new bike Santa brought him for Christmas."

"He most certainly will," laughed Emma.

Chapter 18

*G*ina remained busy through the days of winter with teaching, attending grief counseling sessions, and volunteering at the Pregnancy Counseling Center. She noticed that a peace had begun to settle deep in her soul. How she wanted that for Emma as well. Gina knew the peace she now had came from the assurance that God was in control and had good things planned for her life. He had pursued her through the years with His relentless love. It was only when she fully surrendered to Him once again that she experienced His abiding peace and presence. Mattie had helped her realize that.

Gazing out the window, Gina noticed the first signs that heralded spring's imminent arrival. She noted how the daffodils didn't need any encouragement to bloom. They simply did what they were created to do. *What they were created to do*. She had heard that message repeated in one form or another over and over again, beginning with Bart.

Gina had been pondering Barbara's suggestion about sharing the story of her own pregnancy, her indecision as what to do, then the outcome. Gina felt encouraged by seeing other women choose life, especially Lydia. It took courage for her to tell her parents the situation, then follow through with the decision she had made. Lydia undoubtedly experienced ridicule from her peers. She had stopped by earlier in the week with her own little bundle, baby Rose. What a precious baby, and the look of adoration on Lydia's face was nearly indescribable.

Yes, maybe this was the time Gina should begin writing about her own journey—all stages of it, from life to death. Gina moved to her laptop and opened a blank document. Before she knew it, several pages were written; it seemed as though the words flew off the page.

Her phone rang while she was lost in thought. "Hello," she said somewhat distractedly.

"Gina, are you okay? You sound a little off."

"Hi Abby, I'm just writing—that's all."

Gina proceeded to tell Abby how Barbara at the Pregnancy Counseling Center had encouraged her months ago to write her story, the story of choosing life rather than abortion. Gina finally felt compelled to do so.

"I think seeing Lydia this week with her little one was the deciding factor for me in tackling this. Whether I choose to share it with anyone I'll have to see."

"I can't wait to read it, and I'm so glad that you decided to do so."

Returning to her laptop, Gina reread what she had written: *All life is precious, though there are times we fail to recognize it.* She continued on relating her own story as a single, 25-year-old woman who found herself pregnant, a boyfriend who insisted that she terminate the pregnancy, and the conflicting feelings she felt at that time.

Search your heart and soul before making any life-altering decisions. If I hadn't done that and chose to keep my baby, I would have missed out on so much joy, but others' lives would have been impacted as well. Gina paused momentarily, thinking about Rob, Russell, Emma, Natalie, and yes, even Kellie. *Oh, Lord, I shudder to think of the other outcomes each one of them would have faced, as well as my own.*

While Gina couldn't share what Bart had revealed to her that day in Chico, she remembered other instances when her son had made a difference. *Hmmm,* she thought, *which ones should I include?* There had been so many acts of kindness over the years, or times when Mattie had encouraged others. Fingers resting on her keyboard, an elderly woman named Belle came to mind. Belle adored Mattie, and Mattie felt likewise about Belle. She began typing:

Gina woke with a start, glancing at the clock. "Ugh, 6 o'clock already! Why didn't Mattie awaken me?"

Gina hurried into the baby's room and was surprised by the little one lying on his back. "Look at you! When did you learn to do that?" she exclaimed. A big smile crossed his tiny face.

"Come on, we're going to get you ready to see Belle. You know how much she loves seeing you!" Gina swept Mattie up in her arms and carried him to the changing table.

Belle had been a regular attendee at the Baptist Church Gina's mom attended. Gina had met Belle years ago. While Gina seldom set foot in church anymore, save for Easter and Christmas, Gina kept that connection with Belle alive. She would occasionally stop by on days off from teaching to visit her.

Knocking at the entry, Gina was greeted by an elderly woman who shuffled to the door dressed in a blue housecoat. "Good morning, Belle. Look who I brought by to see you!"

The elderly woman peered through her wire-rim glasses. A bright smile lit up her wizened face. "How is the little one today?"

"He's doing just fine," replied Gina. "He rolled over by himself from his tummy to his back. Was he ever excited about that! Weren't you, Mattie?" she said, handing the small bundle to the older woman to hold.

These visits had begun unexpectedly. Belle was an elderly woman Gina knew who was homebound, with the exception of an occasional outing. Gina began stopping by periodically with Mattie for visits. Before she knew it, they had become routine. Gina wasn't sure who enjoyed them more—Belle or herself.

During those times, the older woman held and rocked the baby. Gina listened as Belle recounted her own life as a young mother back in Pennsylvania, and the struggles she had experienced during the Depression. Gina, likewise, had her own challenges being a single mother and trying to make ends meet. In spite of being the sole caregiver and provider for herself and her young son, Gina wouldn't trade that for anything. Just gazing upon Mattie brought her such joy. Gina could see that the elderly woman felt similarly.

"Let me show you the quilt I've been making for Mattie," Belle said. She pulled out a partially completed top of red, white, and blue. "It's called 'Stars for Patrick' but I'm changing it to 'Stars for Mattie.'" The older woman smiled as she smoothed out her work. "I want it finished by Christmas to give him."

"Oh, Belle, it's going to be lovely! Thank you!" Gina enthused. She rose and wrapped her arms around her elderly friend. "You are such a dear to think of Mattie." Gina knew that Belle subsisted on a meager income. Gifts from her were always handmade with lots of love, but weren't those the best kind of gifts, anyway?

"Ok, in you go," said Gina as she buckled Mattie into his car seat for a few more errands. Saturdays were always busy prepping for the week ahead, with work and taking him to daycare. While expenses were high and a baby added to it, somehow Gina managed to pay bills each month and occasionally have a bit left over. "Mattie, I have no idea how this has happened," Gina said, eyeing her checkbook balance. "I guess someone is looking out for us."

❦

Finishing her thoughts, Gina wrote: *This baby brought joy to an elderly woman who received very little in her daily life. Similarly, her kindness touched the life of my son as well as my own. While this simple act may seem inconsequential to most, it brought purpose to the life of another.*

A second image came to mind of Mattie, around the age of three.

"Momma, Mom!" yelled Mattie.

"What's up, honey?" Gina sat up in bed, where she had been enjoying a few extra minutes of rest.

Mattie toddled into the room with a bowl brimming over with Cheerios. He left a trail of them behind him as he made his way to her. "This is for you, because I love you," he gushed.

Gina grabbed the young boy and pulled him close to her. "And I love you, too!" Such emotion welled up in her heart for this dear one she had been blessed with. So many times she had felt impatient with Mattie and his endless questions and messes. And yet she couldn't imagine life without him.

A smile crossed Gina's face at that sweet remembrance. "Maybe I shouldn't include that; let each woman experience her own moments of joy."

Walking to the mantel in her family room, Gina admired the photo of Emma, Travis, and Mattie that Emma had given her for Christmas. Their faces glowed with happiness. Next to that one sat Gina's all-time favorite of Mattie at six months of age with his toothless grin.

Gina looked down at the photo of her wee one. She thought of the many years that had passed with Mattie. She recalled that day so long ago when she learned that she was pregnant, and the decision she had almost made. "What if you'd never been born?" she asked herself. How would her life be different? She shuddered to think of the possibilities: The little boy who'd brought her so much joy with his endless smiles and kindness to others. The man that little boy had grown into. Each year of his life, Mattie had made countless deposits into the lives of others. By the world's standards they were not significant, but those deposits had changed the outcome of so many lives, especially her own.

"Yes, Lord, you blessed me so many years ago." A tear slid down her face as she thought of the decision she had almost made.

※※※※ ※※※※

Over a period of several weeks, a book of sorts came together. Abby became Gina's writing coach and chief editor, offering suggestions along the way.

When Gina finally felt Mattie's story was finished, she called Abby. "I think it's done. Will you read it one last time, please?"

"You don't have to beg. Of course I'll read it. Have you decided on a title for it?"

"Yes, I plan to call it *Mattie's Story.*"

※※※※ ※※※※

Saturday morning, Abby came by to read the finished manuscript. Walking in the front door, she said, "I smell something tantalizing. What is it?"

"I made cinnamon cranberry muffins. There's coffee, too. An editor does need to be fed and taken care of."

"While I can't argue with that thinking, it will take me more than fifteen minutes to reread this."

"That's why there's food to fuel the journey ahead," laughed Gina.

Abby settled down on the couch with her coffee and Gina's final draft. Gina left her alone and went into another room to catch up on some schoolwork she had set aside.

A couple of hours later, Gina heard Abby calling for her.

"Do you need more coffee?" asked Gina.

"No, thanks honey. I'm done. This is good, I mean really good. Tears were streaming down my face while reading it. You added a bit that wasn't in your earlier version."

"I did. And thanks, I appreciate your vote of confidence."

"You do plan to show this to Barbara, don't you?"

"Yes. I'll make a copy for her and see what she thinks. Even if Barbara doesn't want to use it at the center, it's okay. I think this has been a cathartic process for me."

Wrapping her arms around her friend, Abby said, "I'm so glad."

"Me too. I do have one more thing to do," Gina added somewhat mysteriously.

Chapter 19

Gina sat in Barbara's office at the Pregnancy Counseling Center.

This is beginning to feel like home, she thought. Gina looked around, noticing the prints on the wall that evoked a sense of peace. She especially liked the one that showed a grove of barren trees with the following written beside it: *You were given this life because you are strong enough to live it.* She didn't see the author's name next to it, but at this point in her life, she could honestly say that she agreed with whoever wrote it.

Barbara entered with a cheery hello, noting the stack of papers sitting in Gina's lap. "Is that what I think it is?"

"Yes. It's finished, or at least I believe so. If you can use it as a resource here, I'd be happy to let you do so."

"Gina, I can't wait to read it. Give me a few days and I'll give you a call letting you know my thoughts." Barbara eyed the title: *Mattie's Story.* "I'm sure this wasn't easy to write."

"No, it wasn't. There were plenty of tears associated with it."

"Gina, I am so proud of you and the courage you showed tackling this. You are an inspiration, that's for sure."

"Wait till you read it before you decide whether I'm an inspiration or not," laughed Gina.

⤜⤜⤜

The following day, Gina's cell phone buzzed; looking at caller ID, Gina noticed it was Barbara calling.

"Hi Barbara. I'm surprised to hear from you so soon."

"I started reading *Mattie's Story* last night and couldn't put it down. I stayed up until two this morning, so I'm a bit bleary-eyed."

"And?"

"Gina, your story is very compelling; I think it would be a significant factor in our fight for life. It needs to be published."

"Do you really think so?"

"Yes, I do. Also, we have our annual fundraiser/dinner coming up in a couple of months. I want you to consider sharing this with those attending."

"Barbara, I don't know…."

"Think about it. Meanwhile I'm going to call a friend who works with a publishing company and see what he can do to help publish your story."

Gina felt dazed. Things were happening so quickly, she hardly had time to think. Hadn't she already determined to use her gifts as Bart had admonished her to do? "Then why the hesitation?" she asked herself.

As if answering her own question, a thought popped into her head, *Because it will open you up to the hurt and pain all over again.*

That was it. Reliving all those months of grieving, coming to terms with her loss, and trying to move on. Yet, if she didn't accept Barbara's proposal, wouldn't everything be for naught? She knew what she had to do, regardless of how painful it might be for her.

"Barbara, go ahead with the phone call. And yes, I will share my story at the fundraiser."

After hanging up with Barbara, Gina called Abby. When Abby picked up, Gina related the conversation she had with Barbara. "Can you believe she wants to publish it? That she thinks it's good enough to do so?"

"Yes, I can believe it. I told you myself that I felt it was well done. Gina, you have been volunteering at the Pregnancy Counseling Center for months; this may be just what you need to persuade other women to choose life."

"Barbara said the same thing, more or less."

"I can't wait to see the story in print. I will most certainly buy a copy, and I want it autographed by the author herself."

"Promise," laughed Gina.

<hr>

The following weeks were busy ones. Besides work and Gina's usual outside activities, she helped decide on a cover for *Mattie's Story* and rehearsed the comments she would share at the fundraiser dinner. She felt a growing excitement rather than the dread she normally experienced when asked to address a large group. *How would the group respond?* she wondered.

Gina once again sat at her laptop on a Saturday morning, gazing at the profusion of color outside. Second only to June, May was her favorite month of the year. Gina delighted in the splotches of color everywhere, along with the cheerful songs the birds sang. She was certain that they shared her delight in the month as well.

It had been nearly a year since she lost her son. Normally Gina's mind would be swimming with all the end-of-year projects at school, but not today. Her perspective had been changing over the past few months on many things. Instead, she tried to focus on what her priorities were: use your "gifting" in whatever ways you can. Gina resolved to do that daily. While she was more successful on some days than others, she tried all the same.

Since finishing *Mattie's Story*, Gina felt the need to continue writing. With so much happening within such a short period of time, Gina wished she could relay all of this to her dear son. Out of this longing, she began composing *Letters to Mattie,* more so for herself than to be shared with others.

As Gina sat there typing, the words seemed to flow off the page; she had so much to tell her son. Gina had spotted the first butterfly of the season while planting pansies in her garden yesterday. She paused from her work to enjoy the beauty and grace of the small creature. It occurred to her that butterflies don't begin in that form; rather, they must undergo a metamorphosis from their grubby beginnings to reach that stage. She wrote:

> *Butterflies are creatures of promise, though you might not realize that at first glance. They begin life as ugly, furry caterpillars, seemingly bound to this earthly world. Through the death of that old self, they become something lovely and*

new. It is only through that passage that this metamorphosis can take place. While in the chrysalis stage, all parts of their former selves have been changed to become something different—a butterfly. They are no longer earthbound; they have wings to soar and can discover their new identity. So it is with us—we must die to the old self. Once our metamorphosis is complete, we too will know our true identity and have wings to soar above this earthly home we are currently tethered to.

Gina felt that she was beginning to understand what Bart had tried to convey to her that day in Aroma Coffee. There is so much more than what we experience daily. "I think I get it," she said out loud, focusing on the beauty beyond her window.

❧❧❧ ❦❦❦

Gina stood at the podium, a bit nervous. Months ago, she never would have foreseen herself speaking to a group of pro-life women. The old Gina would have kept her thoughts to herself. Scanning the crowd for any familiar faces, she smiled when she caught sight of Abby, Emma, and Barbara all seated together. They gave her a thumbs-up. She returned it before glancing once again at her notes. In a clear and confident tone, she stated:

"This is how my journey began." And Gina launched into her own story that took place twenty-six years ago. She shared the uncertainty she felt learning that she was pregnant; the rejection and betrayal she suffered from her boyfriend; the struggles she experienced as a single mom—but most of all, the absolute joy of being a mother. Finally, she described the loss of her son. While that had been devastating, equally devastating would have been the deprivation of never holding him and enjoying his presence over the years, which would have been the outcome had she had the abortion.

Gina concluded by saying, "Each of us is here for a purpose. We have been created for a reason, and have a very specific job to do. Don't let anyone tell you that a life is meaningless; all life has value. As someone once told me, find that purpose that you alone are intended for and pour your heart into it. That is my challenge to each and every one of you here tonight."

As Gina stepped off the podium, an explosion of applause greeted her. She smiled appreciatively.

"Thank you, Mattie," Gina whispered.

Chapter 20

It seemed just like it was yesterday that Gina, family, and friends gathered to say goodbye to Mattie at Chico Cemetery, but in fact a year had already passed. Gina thought back to that day: While somberness filled the ceremony, Gina had an inner peace about her. After the brief encounter with Mattie, she knew that his time on Earth had been lived fully, impacting many lives in the process. More so, Gina understood that Mattie had completed his assignment, what he was created to do. How could anyone feel anything but joy knowing he had done so?

A year already, so hard to believe, not to mention the journey each one of them had taken during that time. Bart had been correct when he admonished Gina to use her gifts, fulfill her purpose for existence. She pondered her own journey over the past months. It would have seemed an unlikely one if someone had suggested it to her before Mattie's passing. Volunteering at the Pregnancy Counseling Center? Writing a book? She learned that the Lord does have a plan for each person's life, and He uses everything that He allows in our lives for good if we release it to Him.

While struggling to forgive the drunk driver who had killed her son, Gina finally was able to let that go as well. She had learned that God would deal with that person as He chose to. Bart made it perfectly clear to Gina that day in Aroma Coffee that God took Mattie home; it wasn't an accident.

Emma, Travis, and Gina stood at Mattie's grave in Chico Cemetery. With another scorcher being forecast for the day ahead, they had arrived early, minutes after the cemetery had opened. Each laid a solitary red rose beneath the headstone that read: Matthew Paul Hensley—*loved by many, a friend to all.* They whispered their own silent prayers, mindful of the serenity surrounding them.

The trio moved away from Mattie's grave. Gina sensed her son's presence once again, encouraging her to continue on the path she had chosen.

"I love the beauty and serenity that is present in this place," Emma said as they headed toward their car.

"I couldn't agree more. It's almost like having a small slice of heaven here on Earth."

"How can heaven be on Earth?" asked Travis.

"Travis, it's just an expression," replied Emma.

"What do all of you think about going to The Bear for an early lunch?" Gina asked. "I believe it's still someone's favorite hangout spot."

"That's a great idea," agreed Travis.

"Alright, then. The Bear it is."

Gina looked at the others and felt an inner peace. She had truly been blessed.

> "Your eyes saw my unformed body; all the days ordained for me were written in your book before one of them came to be." Psalm 139:16

Made in the USA
Las Vegas, NV
18 January 2022

41747354R10081